WILL SPARROW'S ROAD

KAREN CUSHMAN

HOUGHTON MIFFLIN HARCOURT
BOSTON NEW YORK

www.hmhco.com

The text of this book is set in ITC Veljovic.

The Library of Congress has cataloged the hardcover edition as follows:
Will Sparrow's road / Karen Cushman.
p.   cm.
Summary: In 1599 England, twelve-year-old lying, thieving Will Sparrow runs away,
meets many colorful characters on the road, and then reluctantly joins a traveling
"oddities" exhibit, where he learns to see beyond appearances.
[1. Conduct of life—Fiction. 2. Freak shows—Fiction. 3. Runaways—Fiction.
4. Great Britain—History—Elizabeth, 1558–1603—Fiction.] I. Title.
PZ7.C962Wil   2012
[Fic]—dc23
2011045898

ISBN: 978-0-547-73962-5 hardcover
ISBN: 978-0-544-33632-2 paperback

Manufactured in the United States of America
DOC 10 9 8 7 6 5 4 3 2 1

4500500402

For all those who asked,

"Will you ever write a book about a boy?"

With thanks to

Merna Hecht for the sensitivity discussions,

Kirby Larson and Dorothy Love for their encouragement and their example,

the librarians of King County, Washington,

for books and more books,

the legendary Dinah Stevenson for wisdom, jots, and quibbles,

and

Philip for love, for unfailing support,

and for being the perfect model of a twelve-year-old boy

SOMEWHERE IN ENGLAND, THE YEAR 1599

# ONE

INTRODUCING WILL SPARROW,

NOT YET THIRTEEN BUT ALONE AND

ON THE ROAD TO NOWHERE

WILL SPARROW was a liar and a thief, and hungry, so when he saw the chance to steal a cold rabbit pie from the inn's kitchen and blame it on the dog, he took it—both the chance and the pie. But the innkeeper would have none of it: "And how did the wee dog open the door, scrabble onto the table, and fetch the pie out of the kitchen, all the while sitting on Mistress Grubb's lap having his ears scratched, I would like to know?" He grabbed Will by the shoulders and shook him. Pie-crust crumbs fell like snow.

"Ye have stolen your last meal, boy. I paid too high a price for you," the innkeeper said with a spray of spittle. "Free drink for your lout of a father. I could easily hire me two boys for what he costs me in ale."

Will struggled to escape, but the innkeeper held on tighter. "No, boy, you be liar and thief and not worth your keep. I mean to send you to the city. Sell you for a climbing boy."

Will's heart thumped. A chimney sweep? "Nay," he said, still struggling. "Ne'er!"

"Aye, boy. There always be a market for such," the innkeeper continued. "Them don't last long. They lungs go."

Will kicked his captor in the knee and, shoving the table aside, turned for the door, but the innkeeper stuck out a booted foot, sending Will tumbling to the ground.

"You be off with the carter in the morning," he said, lifting Will by the collar of his shirt.

Although Will struggled and kicked and tried to bite the innkeeper's large and leathery arm, he could not escape and was locked in the stable—without his boots, lest he run. But it is difficult to keep a wiry, clever, sad, and angry lad locked up, and Will worked on the boards of the stable, making first a mousehole, and then a hole a weasel might fit through, and finally a hole large enough for a small but determined boy. He wrapped a blanket, prickly with horsehair and straw but not too tattered for warmth, around his shoulders. Exhaling loudly, he squeezed through the hole and ran into the night.

In the deepening dark, the boy could not see the

road ahead, so he ran with his arms outstretched and waving wildly, lest he collide with a tree or a wagon or some unknown frightful thing. Such motions made running difficult and slow, but no one could follow him in the dark, so he ran.

Finally his arms and shoulders, not to mention his legs and feet, grew so tired and ached so fiercely that he had to take the risk and stop. Where he was he did not know. On the road or off, he did not know. The darkness and the strangeness frightened him, and his heart beat like a tambour. He moved forward until he felt something—a tree stump, he guessed—by which he could rest without fear of being overrun by a cart or trampled by a horse. Lying down, he snuggled into the blanket, his back against the stump, for that way he felt less lonesome and forlorn.

The night was full of sounds. Leaves rustled and whispered, the wind moaned, branches creaked and snapped. Will could not sleep. He lay imagining the innkeeper catching him, his father finding him, or—worse—trolls and goblins, ogres and elves and evil dwarfs, come out of the forest to bedevil him. When he heard the direful hooting of an owl, he pulled the blanket over his head. Finally, comforted by the familiar smell of horse, he slept.

Dawn comes early in summer, so before long he

woke to the sound of a cockcrow and opened his eyes. Fie upon it! In the dark he had doubled back and was now not an hour's walk from where he'd started. He smiled a sour smile. Leastwise the innkeeper would not be looking for him here, so near to the inn.

He rubbed his eyes, washed his face, and drank deeply from a stream running warm and shallow. "You, Will Sparrow," he said to his face shimmering in the water, "are a sorry excuse for a runabout. Now you must start again."

When folk heard his name, they smiled at first, it being a fitting name for one so small and brown, but then, thinking "Sparrow? Sparrow?" some would remember his father, the drunken fool who sold his only son for ale, and would turn away in disgust. So Will ran, from the innkeeper and the carter, from his ale-sodden father, from the disapproving faces of folk, from his very life.

Will's stomach was empty, his head fuzzy, his legs heavy. He could go no more until he fed them all. Slowly he picked his way along the road, careful to keep the hedgerow between himself and anyone's eyes. It being late summer, he found a thorny thicket of blackberries, shiny and plump and smelling of sunshine, which he picked until his hands were purple and ate until his belly threatened to give them all up.

He wiped his hands on his breeches and stretched.

While he ate, the road had grown busy with travelers in fancy cloaks and threadbare linen, carts and coaches and hay wagons, horses and sheep, merchants and beggars. Even with the shelter of the hedgerow, Will thought himself too easily seen and found. But where might he go? To his right was ploughland, golden with ripened grain, and to his left deep forest. In the forest he might be hidden from sight, but it was a dark and evil place, filled with demons and beasts and men who lived like beasts.

"You, boy," someone called, and without stopping to see who called or who was meant, Will hitched up his breeches and his courage and ran into the woods. Brambles tore at his legs, branches whipped his face and tugged at his hair, but fear drove him on, away from the inn and toward he knew not what.

Was he running east or west? Toward a town or away? Was the innkeeper still looking for him? Had he sent the carter to fetch Will back? And his father—did his father care enough to search for him? Was the man too codswalloped to follow? Or had he lost his chance at free ale when Will ran, which would leave him sober and storming? Will shivered at the thought. Being sober enraged his father, as did honking geese, beggars, bill collectors, and Will himself.

The innkeeper had been no easier than Will's father,

but at the inn Will was fed somewhat regularly and many an extra sausage found its way under his shirt and into his belly, so he had stayed while wet spring turned to high summer. He slept in the stable behind the inn and each morning turned the spit on which joints of meat roasted, scoured the pots the mutton stew simmered in, and gathered up the rushes befouled with bones, grease, and piss, until that pilfered rabbit pie undid him.

He ran all morning, eager to put as much distance as possible between himself and the inn. By midafternoon the day was so bright that streaks of sunshine found their way even through the trees. He would have to hide until evening. He found a small hollow to curl into, pulled the blanket over himself for cover, and fell soundly asleep.

He awoke not long after to whistles and shouts. "I am certain he went this way," a rumbly voice called.

Will froze.

"I will go this way and you that. He cannot get away," said a scratchy voice.

Will crouched lower under the branches. How could they have found him so easily?

"Come, boy. Come out," Rumbly Voice said.

Scratchy Voice shouted in triumph, "There he is! I see him! Come out. You cannot get away."

Will looked about for an escape. He would not be taken so easily, not end up a climbing boy and die sooty and coughing in a chimney.

"Come on, boy. Be not afeared," Scratchy Voice said.

As he dove into the brambles, Will heard a soft nickering. "Good boy," said Rumbly Voice. "I have a carrot for ye."

Will stopped and peeked through the bushes. A horse was poking its way toward two men. One of them slipped a halter over the horse's neck and patted its rump. "Good boy, good. No one will hurt ye," the man rumbled. Will could hear the sound of carrot crunching. "Come, we will take ye home."

The two men and the horse turned and walked away.

Will slapped his head. A horse. It was a horse they were after and not him at all! He was dizzy with relief but did envy the horse the carrot, the gentle words, and the home. Will himself had no prospect for any of those. He turned back for his blanket and then walked on.

It appeared to Will as if the woods went on forever, even to the edge of the earth where there were monsters and dragons. He shivered but walked ahead. There was nothing for him behind.

TWO

OF HOW WILL MOURNED

A LOST BUTTON, A BLANKET,

AND A MOTHER

FTERNOON BECAME gentle dusk. Will filled his belly with berries and dreamed of warm porridge and buttered bread. As he sat for a moment's rest, he heard a scuffling sort of noise. Was it the horse come back? Or had the men returned for him?

The scuffling grew louder and proved to be a deer, eating her way through the forest. Will caught his breath, and the deer cocked her head and twirled her long, rabbitlike ears. In the last rays of light, her reddish-brown coat gleamed. Will stared at her. She was well muscled and a bit plump. *If I could catch her, I could eat her,* he thought. *If I could catch her and skin her and butcher her and gather wood and build a fire and roast her until juicy, I could eat her.* He made a sound between a sigh and a snort—there was little chance of all that. The deer twitched her tail once and was gone. Will picked another handful of berries and resumed his journey.

Berries. He was sick of berries, but he had not seen a cottage to plunder nor a chicken to steal, not even a poacher or a charcoal burner who might be wheedled out of a bit of bread or cheese. Walking became tiring, then tedious, then a torment, and he began searching for something to distract him. "I am the famed highwayman Gamaliel Ratsey," he roared, settling the blanket over his shoulders as if it were a cape, "taking what I want and wanting what I take. I care for no one but myself and nothing but my belly!"

He pulled the blanket over his face. "A dangerous outlaw I be, lurking here in the woods, waiting for unwary travelers to pillage and skewer." But the thought frightened him, there alone in the darkening evening, and he looked carefully around before wrapping the blanket about him like—well, a blanket, and curling up to sleep.

He woke to find he had slept away the cover of darkness but not the pangs of a belly empty once again. As he trudged through the morning, the woods thinned into thickets, then hedges, then a road lined with avenues of trees—hawthorn, birch, alder, ash, apple. Apple? Apples! Will saw no one to stop him, so he scampered up the closest tree. It was heavy with apples, speckled and freckled and more green than red but there for the taking, so Will took them. *Like Ratsey,* he thought, *I care for no one but myself and nothing but my belly.* He liked the sound of that, so he said it aloud, but not too loud, lest he be heard and caught: "I care for no one but myself and nothing but my belly!"

He loaded apples onto his blanket and slid carefully down from the tree. Slinging the blanket over his shoulder, he took a large bite of an apple, which crackled and spewed sweet juice. Too bad trees did not also bear cheese, he thought. Or chickens. Or almond tarts.

The forest had thinned enough to offer little cover, and walking on the road would be easier and gentler on his bare feet. It would be worth the risk, he decided. Not knowing the direction he had come from, he did not know whither he should go. Finally he shrugged and turned to his left, where the road led over a hill and down, munching as he walked.

As the afternoon wore on, a summer rain, blustery and heavy, began. Hooded shepherds drove soggy sheep through the meadows, and laborers hurriedly gathered grain ere it was ruined in the wet.

The rain meant there were fewer people about to notice him, but Will grew sodden and sorry, and he finally looked for refuge. In a field of lean, tired-faced cattle was what appeared to be a cowshed, near to tumbling down but offering at least walls and a roof.

The floor of the shed was carpeted with old straw, which smelled strongly of cow and horse and rat. The straw was damp with what Will hoped was only rain, but mostly the shed was dry, and he would be off the road there and hidden. Hanging from a nail on the wall was a canvas sack, which he took down and filled with his apples. He pulled off his wet shirt and wrung it out. The button was gone from the collar. It must have happened when the innkeeper grabbed him. Will mourned the button—not everyone had a shirt with a button. He pictured the button bouncing onto the floor of the inn and into a crack, never to be seen again. Or mayhap picked up by a visitor, who put it into the pouch at his waist with a prayer of thanks to whatever saint had sent him so fine a thing as a button.

He sighed as he hung the shirt from the nail to dry and, spreading his blanket on a pile of straw, lay down to sleep, soothed by the rhythm of the rain on the roof.

Awakened after minutes or hours, he did not know which, Will heard the sound of someone coming into the shed. He jumped up, shouting, "Avaunt ye! Go away! I have a sword!" and prepared to hurl apples at the intruder, but a sudden glimmer of moonlight peeping through the cracks in the walls showed him it was a woman. The innkeeper would not have sent a woman after him, Will thought, so he dropped the apples back into the sack, though he stood still and wary.

"Quite a palace you have here, boy," the woman said. "I have in mind to share it, an it please you. It be raining fit for Noah out there." She did not wait for his agreement but threw herself onto a pile of straw. "Who might you be and what do you here?"

Will said nothing but backed up and held tightly to his sack of apples.

"Skittish, are you, boy? I mean you no harm."

Still Will did not answer.

"Nay, do not leave me in silence," the strange woman said. "I am wet and tired and would have some amusement. You had best talk to me, or I will tousle your hair and tickle your toes and generally bedevil you as I did my brothers." She laughed loudly. "I be Nell Liftpurse."

"Liftpurse? You be a nipper!" Will said, startled into responding. And he held tighter to his sack.

"Some say nipper. Some say pickpocket. I say I do but take advantage of opportunities . . . and I be most nimble." She lifted her hand and waggled her fingers. Her hand was marked with a *T,* branded into the flesh. *T* for *thief,* no matter what she said, thought Will. He himself was too clever and too slippery to be caught ever again. He was Will Sparrow, liar and thief. Still, he looked at his own hand holding the sack and rubbed it gently.

"Now tell me," Nell Liftpurse said, "who be you and what do you in a cowshed?"

Unwilling to be tickled or tousled, Will, with a grimace of reluctance, finally told her his name. Then he gulped. What if she had been sent to find him? Or mayhap she would later meet someone who sought him? Here he was, telling his name to strangers in cowsheds. Some poor runaway he was! He shook his head. He had spoken already, so "I be on an errand for my father," he told her, "and, like you, found shelter from the rain." It sounded convincing enough. "My father be, uhh, sheriff, aye, sheriff of this county, very rich and very powerful, and I be his most treasured son."

The rain still pelted down, and Will was in no hurry to be on the road again, so he dropped onto the straw and put his sack of apples behind his head like a pillow. Wrapped in the blanket, he studied Nell Liftpurse. Even in the poor light, she looked a colorful person: plump red face, white teeth, sky-blue kirtle under a bodice of buttercup yellow, and fine reddish hair peeping out from beneath a soggy green hat. And boots, sturdy boots of heavy leather. Will's bare feet tingled at the sight of those boots as she pulled them off and wiggled her toes with an "Aaah." Mayhap she would fall asleep, and the boots could find their way onto his feet and out the door and her all unaware. Will Sparrow, clever and slippery, liar and thief, would have those boots.

Nell threw the boots behind her, leaned over, and thumped Will on the knee. "Where you goin' to?"

"Nowhere," he said, tugging his mind away from her boots. "I be goin' from."

"A runner, are ye? Least little thing goes wrong and ye run."

Will's temper boiled over. He sat up and grabbed the bag of apples. "'Little thing,' you say? My father traded me to an innkeeper for beer. That be no little thing." Will's anger was mingled with an odd bit of pride: certes no other father in the world misprized his son so.

"My own daddy, he ne'er would have done as yours did," Nell said, lying back in the straw. "We lost our land when the scurvy lord took it. He dammed the river, and the whole village disappeared beneath a lake he used for mock sea battles. We was eight and no mam, but ne'er did my daddy think to rid himself of us." Nell frowned and was silent for a bit. "Your own father, you say? May turnips grow in his nose! Why, had I a son like you, a brave and bonny boy, I would ne'er treat him so." She slammed her fist against the straw-strewn floor. "Were the man here," she declared, "I would cuff him about his ears, I would."

She panted in outrage for a moment and then asked, "What be in that sack you're cuddling like a babe? 'Twouldn't be someut to eat, would it?"

Will clutched his sack of apples. "Nay, 'tis nothing. Only the . . . the remains of . . . of . . . a cat. An old cat. I did pledge to my dear granny that I would bury her cat . . . er, in a sunny place. Aye, in a sunny place by a stream, and so I will."

Nell still looked curiously at the sack, so Will added, "He do be starting to stink some."

Nell shivered and waved him silent. His apples, Will thought, were safe.

Of a sudden there were voices calling in the field outside. Nell jumped up. "Do someone seek ye?" she asked.

Did they? Will shrugged, then nodded, then shrugged again. Was the innkeeper still on his trail? Or the carter?

"I aim to hide myself, boy," Nell said, "burrow into that straw like a mole. You might do the same, and they will find no one here." She gave him a small shove. "Go. God save ye, boy," she said. She shook her head. "Traded for beer, the poor wee wretch."

Will slipped into his shirt, still damp from the rain, and crouched in the corner, pulling great masses of straw over himself. He would hide just long enough for the voices to pass, and then, before Nell showed herself again, he would have her boots and be off. Will was grateful for her sympathy, but boots were boots.

Pieces of straw poked in his mouth and tickled his nose. A sneeze began, and grew, and grew. Will muffled it with his arm, but then came another and another. He wiped his soggy hand on his breeches and waited. Had he given himself away?

The voices outside came nearer, and Will heard someone say, "Mayhap the baggage is in the shed." And the door swung open and shut.

Had they come in? Will's heart pounded so loudly, he was certain it could be heard even to the next county. Belike he would be back at the inn before morning. His belly grumbled at the thought.

There came a shout from outside. "There she goes!"

And another: "Nellie, girl, we got you now. Nellie! Nell?"

"Blast it," said the first voice. "Where has the she-devil gone?" and their voices grew fainter as they moved off.

Will was bewildered. Gone? She was gone? Was she not hiding in the straw? He stood up, brushing straw from his hair and his clothes and his mouth. He was alone. The men had not come *in*. She had run *out*. And they had called her Nell. They were after her all along and not him! Horses and thieves were worth following and recovering, but he was not, it appeared.

He looked around the shed. Nell was gone indeed, and so too were her boots. And his blanket and the sack of apples. Gone, the lying thief, the villainous harpy, may maggots build nests in her hair!

He opened the door and peered out. No one was there waiting for him, so he stepped outside. "Begone and stay gone, you baggage!" he shouted. "I hope my apples gripe your guts and rats eat your toes right through those fine boots!"

It appeared Will Sparrow was not the clever thief he thought himself, for he was left with no boots, no apples, no blanket. Outsmarted by a woman! Nell had acted kindly toward him and then stole what little he had, the foul and ugly toad. Fie upon it, he would not make that mistake again. He would speak to no one, listen to no one, and let no one get close enough to take what was his. *I care for no one but myself,* he thought, kicking at the straw-covered floor, *and nothing but my belly. And boots.*

Fie on Nell Liftpurse, the hag! Fie on all women! He had nothing good to say for them. His mother had run off when he was small enough still to need a mother. No more than five he was when she left, the selfish wretch. Will hated her and hoped she was grown ugly, crooked, and wartish.

His stepmother, the green-eyed Ysabo, who had

appeared before his mother's chair was cold, had left them soon after for the miller, who was pockmarked and stooped but had promised her two new dresses and fresh bread every week. She told Will so before she left, their last chicken under her arm.

He hated both of them but especially his mother, with her silver gilt hair and her soft laughter. Fie upon her! Thinking of his mother grizzled his liver, so he shut the memories away as if in a cupboard and locked them in.

Will felt the dawn chill on his face. It was time to go. The rain had stopped, and the fading moon was yet bright enough to light his way. He was far enough from the inn, he thought, that it would be safe to walk on the road as long as he kept his wits about him.

Snuffling loudly, he kicked at a puddle. No one was seeking him here. He was not worth that much to the innkeeper and worth nothing to his tall, redheaded father, the Devil take him! Village schoolmaster the man had been, insufficiently learned though handy with the switch, but a man of some consequence until his wife left and he took to drink, forfeiting his position and his friends and his prospects. " 'Tis your fault she be gone," Will's father told him often. "She could not abide you, and no more can I. Look at you, you dark, skinny runt. I mistrust you are mine. A changeling, most like, left by

fairies when they took my own son. My real boy . . ."
He mewled and blubbered like a babe, lost himself in
drink, boxed Will about the ears regularly, and sold him
to the innkeeper.

Will picked up a rock and hurled it at the nearest
tree. He was no changeling! Will hurled another rock.
Although he was not tall and redheaded, nor soft and
silver haired, but small and dark, he was no changeling. He was Will Sparrow, wary and sly, liar and thief,
with knobby knees and a gap-toothed smile. He could
whistle through that gap, spit through it, and thrust the
tip of his tongue through it when he thought or wondered or worried, as he did now.

Will was alone, farther from home than he had ever
been, with no plan, no one to depend on, no one to
trust. He took a deep breath of the rain-washed air. In
sooth, everything lay ahead of him. He was no inn boy,
no chimney sweep. He was free and on the road to
somewhere. A tiny flicker of hope flared in his belly.

THREE

IN WHICH WILL EARNS

BUT IS CHEATED OF A SUPPER

THE DAY grew hot and late-summer dry, and the puddles disappeared in the sun. Tired of walking and weary in his bones, Will trudged through the brown grass. *Scritch-scritcha-scritch,* it sang as he walked, and he was suddenly attentive. *Scritch-scritcha-scritch.* If he put one dirty bare foot on the road and the other in the grass, he could change the tune: *thud-scritcha-thud.*

By moving back and forth from grass to road, he could make music: *scritch-scritcha-thud-thud, thud-scritcha-thud. Bump-bumpa* went a rock as he kicked it, and Will added that to his song. *Scritch-scritcha-thud-thud, thud-scritcha-thud-bump-bumpa.* He chanted it aloud as he walked: *Scritch-scritcha-thud-thud, thud-scritcha-thud, bump-bumpa-bump-bump.*

So intent was he on his music making that he nearly walked into a wagon parked at the side of the road.

"Watch yourself, boy," a voice said, "or you will end up with a bump-bumpa-bump-bump on that head of yours."

Will stopped, ready to run, but saw from the corner of his eye what appeared to be a giant tooth wobbling in the breeze. Surely his pursuers would not chase him in a wagon topped with a giant tooth.

"I see you admiring my embellishments," said the man with the voice, who was standing next to the toothed wagon. He was shaped much like an egg: small at the top and bottom and rounded in the middle, stuffed into a padded doublet of stained and spotted green. "I be Doctor Hieronymus Munster," he said with a little bow, "tooth puller and traveling purveyor of remedies. Need you extraction or distraction or satisfaction, I can likely provide."

Will said nothing and resumed walking. The man was not the innkeeper nor the carter who would take him to sweep chimneys, but as likely as not he was up to no good. Will's encounter with Nell Liftpurse had taught him that wary as he was, clever and slippery as he was, it was not enough for a boy in a world of grown-up liars and thieves.

The man climbed onto the wagon. He clucked to

his great black horse, and they drove slowly alongside the boy. "From the appearance of your dusty attire and your dirty feet, I suspect you would not be disinclined to ride to wherever you are headed," said the man. "Do I have the way of it?"

Will's tired feet pleaded, "Aye, aye, we want to ride," but the boy shook his head.

"Be you mute or merely thrifty with your words?"

"I can speak," said Will, "when I have reason," but he did not stop.

"Good. I wish to come to an agreeance with you. I seek your aid, if you'd care to—"

"Nay, I care for no one but myself and nothing but my belly."

"A prudent stance, I do say. But I have business awaiting in a village yon, and, if you will assist me, I will remunerate you."

Will crinkled his face in puzzlement. Was that a threat? Should he run?

"*Pay,* boy. That means I will pay you," said the man.

Pay? Will stopped. "How much?" he asked. "Show me."

"I do not precisely have the coins now," the man said, and Will shook his head again and walked on. "But with your help, I shall be earning a great many, which

I shall use to buy us supper. Juicy fat beef ribs. Pork pies. And crumb cakes."

Will slowed. He had seen fine folk eat such at the inn, but he himself had had only the leavings.

"We shall sit by the fire and eat our fill," said the tooth puller.

"With new bread? And mugs of ale?" It was more than he had hoped for, willing to be satisfied by smoked herring or jellied eels.

"Certes," the man said, nodding his head until his chins wobbled.

"What you would have me do—be it painful, gruesome, or disgustful?"

"Not at all. You will merely serve as an exemplar of my work."

Will did not understand what that meant, but since it was not painful, gruesome, or disgustful, he said, "I might, if I choose." He walked even slower. "And there will be beef ribs afterward?"

The tooth puller nodded again.

"Then 'tis possible I will do it," Will said, still wary of the man but eager to feel the grease of the beef on his lips.

"Climb up, then, young master," said Doctor Hieronymus Munster, and Will did.

The man shook the reins, and the big black horse began to move. "Where be you headed?" he asked.

Will motioned vaguely toward the road ahead. "Up there."

"Good," said Doctor Munster. "That is precisely where I am going."

"What is it you will pay me to do? You do not expect me to pull teeth as you do?"

Doctor Munster chuckled. "Pish, as if a slip of a boy like you could pull out anything more difficult than a fish from a stream. You will only show folk how easy and painless it be to have a tooth drawn."

"You mean to pull my teeth?" Will made ready to leap from the wagon.

"Nay, nay, not in truth, but it will appear so. You will be doing folk a boon, calming their fears and assuring them of the safety and painlessness of the procedure."

"You mean I shall lie," Will said, nodding. "That I can do."

"Lie? Lie? I never thought of it as lying, more as . . . representing and . . . encouraging. I often use some lackwit fellow I pick up—" The doctor stopped talking and cleared his throat. "Nay, *usually* I use a lackwit fellow, but you seem a bright and likely boy." Handing the reins to Will, the tooth puller put his hand into his own mouth, clutched a front tooth with his fingers, tugged a bit, and held up a bloody tooth.

Will nearly dropped the reins. How had the man done that? How could he pull out a tooth with his fingers? And the blood—did it not hurt?

Then the tooth puller smiled. His tooth was still there.

"But I saw you pull that tooth with my own eyes," Will said.

"Things are not always what they seem, boy." The tooth puller put the tooth in his pouch and took the reins back from Will. "It takes but practice and a bit of chicken blood. Now let me hear you moan."

"Moan?" Will asked. "Why moan?" Again he made ready to flee if he liked not the answer.

"If you are to assist me, you must seem so distraught with pain that you have come to me to have your tooth removed. Now moan."

Will frowned. He would not perform like a trained dog at a fair. Even so, at the thought that he might lose the beef ribs and warm bread, he moaned, *"Ohhhhhh."* He coughed a bit from the dust as they bounced and swayed down the road, and he moaned again, *"Ohhhhhh."*

"Just so," said the tooth puller, "but louder. Think of some injury you have suffered."

Will thought of the time he ripped the nail off his toe as he was climbing the stone fence around Odo Waterman's orchard, and he moaned louder.

"Good," said the tooth puller. "Now make it a bit deeper."

Will remembered slamming his finger in the door of the inn the day he arrived. The finger dangled broken and useless until Magda the midwife forced it straight and tied it tightly with two sticks and a length of cloth torn from her underskirt. Will moaned deeper.

"Better, better, but with more pain."

Will considered the time his father sent him to catch a fish for their supper and Will lay on the bank, his feet dangling in the water, enjoying the way the fish nibbled at his toes, until his father found him and cuffed him so hard that he fell and cracked his head on a rock and blood trickled from his ear. Will heard less well on that side now, and sometimes the ear ached fiercely. *"Ahhhh-ehhh-owww!"* Will bellowed.

"A truly prodigious effort, my boy!" Doctor Munster said, slapping his knee. "Now I will pull the tooth from your mouth and hold it aloft. You will give me many good thanks and disappear before anyone do look too closely at your teeth, which will all be there."

They practiced again and again as the wagon slowly rumbled along. By and by, Doctor Munster called, "Whoa,

Molly," and they bounced to a stop. "Here I will ready myself for my entrance into the village."

He climbed down, a curious Will following him. Behind the wagon, the man shrugged into a cloak of russet wool and placed a pointed hat securely on his head. Lastly he settled around his neck a string of rugged brownish stones.

Will looked closely at the string. Not stones but teeth. He shuddered. *Teeth.*

"I am ready," said Hieronymus Munster. "Molly and I will ride into the village, but you must come around through those trees there lest the village folk see us together and grow suspicious. I will set up in the churchyard, and you will meet us there. Do be moaning and staggering from pain when you arrive."

"When do we sup?"

Doctor Munster waved his hand at the boy. "Anon, anon. After you leave the churchyard, come hither. I will meet you when I have finished relieving folks of their teeth and their coins." He lifted from the wagon a small drum and tapped it twice. "Be ready to leave at once. We will depart in some haste, for folk grow testy when they discover tooth pulling is not as easy or painless as promised. Then we shall visit a coaching inn I know of that offers the fattest beef and the freshest ale. Now begone. I will see you soonly."

Will patted his empty belly and soothed it with promises: "We hoped for someut to eat besides apples, and here it be. We shall be stuffed full and satisfied ere the day be out." Hope again flickered within him.

He did as he was bid and cut through the trees to the village. Cottages leaned and tumbled on both sides of a dusty road that was playground for children and supper table for chickens. He saw the church some way down the road.

The wagon with its waggling tooth stood nigh a tree stump, where a small crowd was gathering. Doctor Munster was next to the stump, banging his drum and shouting, "Do your teeth trouble you more than the tax collector? Do you fear you will never again bite into a crisp apple or a crust of bread? Do you lie awake by night in sore distress? I can free you from your pain—I, Doctor Hieronymus Munster, trained by masters of the dental arts in far-off Arabia. I have with good success and without pain pulled teeth from the crowned heads of Europe, and I can do the same for you here in this celebrated community of, er . . ." He looked around.

Someone called out, "Lesser Oakbridge."

"Indeed," Doctor Munster continued, "here in Lesser Oakbridge." He beckoned to his listeners. "Come and be made sound again, goodmen and ladies. Be not afeared, be not afeared."

No one came forward, so the tooth puller signaled to Will, who put his hand to his cheek and let out a tremendous moan. "Ah, lad, I hear your suffering. Come up, come up, and experience the painless artistry of Doctor Hieronymus Munster. A shilling to draw forth a stump, or but sixpence if the tooth be whole."

Will moved nearer, and Doctor Munster pushed him down onto the tree stump. "Moan, you lumpish rascal! Moan!" the tooth puller whispered to Will, who moaned. The tooth puller put his hand into the boy's mouth, Will wriggled, and finally Doctor Munster held a bloody tooth above his head. "Success!"

Will felt his teeth with his tongue. They were all there. "Painless?" the tooth puller asked. Will nodded.

The tooth puller whispered, "Go now, boy, make haste." Will nodded again.

People pressed closer and examined the tooth in the tooth puller's hand. "Be there anyone else with pain I can relieve? You see how simple and how quick it be. You, goodman," Doctor Munster said to a gray-bearded man holding his chin, "you look as if you suffer. Only sixpence will see you restored." The man dropped coins into Doctor Munster's outstretched hand and sat down on the tree stump.

The tooth puller slipped the coins into the purse at his waist and took up pliers and a knife. "Open wide," he said. The gray-bearded man opened wide. So did the folk standing near, listening and watching closely. And so, without thinking, did Will, who, intent on watching, had not gone from the churchyard.

Doctor Munster poked and scraped and wrestled the tooth while the graybeard moaned and groaned and squirmed. Finally the tooth puller held a bit of a tooth aloft, but the old man was not relieved. He howled, and the crowd murmured and pointed.

"Sixpence more to remove the stump," said Doctor Munster with his hand out.

Will, fearing what might happen if the crowd turned against the tooth puller, drew closer. "Master Munster," he whispered, "I will take coins instead of beef ribs, and I will take them now."

"Get away, young fool," the tooth puller growled, and he began backing toward his wagon.

"Sir," Will said, "I have done what I was bid, and you promised—"

"Look!" shouted a large woman in russet kirtle and grimy wimple. "Look at the boy! See his teeth! The tooth puller pulled nothing!"

The crowd turned from Munster to Will. Someone grabbed him and forced his mouth open wide, revealing his teeth—large and strong and a bit crooked, with a gap he could whistle through, but all there. "She be right!" the someone cried. "The man took no tooth! He is a fraud! And the boy, too!"

The crowd took up the cry. "Fakes! Frauds!"

Doctor Munster pushed the gray-bearded man away and leapt onto the wagon seat. He took up the reins, and the wagon began to move.

Will twisted away from his captors and ran after him, shouting, "Wait for me! My coins! My supper! Beef, you said, and bread!"

The gray-bearded man ran after Will, crying, "My sixpence! Give me back my sixpence!"

Other folk called, "Fakes! Frauds! Come you back, you rascals, and face our wrath!" But Doctor Munster was whipping Molly out of the town. The giant tooth overhanging the wagon wobbled and swayed.

Puffing and panting, Will cut through the woods to the place where he and Doctor Munster were to meet. He waited. And he waited. The tooth puller did not come.

Will's head felt heavy with weariness and hunger. Finally he knew that the tooth puller was gone and the promised dinner with him. "A pox on you, you lying ratsbane and villainous varlet!" he shouted into the deepening darkness. "May the Devil gnaw your bones!"

Will had seen diners sneak from the inn without paying for their dinners; he had known drinkers to finish someone else's mug, watched folks help themselves to the contents of others' purses. Why had he believed the tooth man to be anything but another kind of thief? Once again he had been deceived. From now on it would be coins first, proof first, Will first!

The air grew cool, but Will was warmed by his anger. His mother, his father, the innkeeper, Nell Liftpurse, the tooth puller—all of humankind, it seemed—were liars and deceivers. None of them could he rely on, none of them had a care for him. *And no more do I care for them,* he added. *I care for no one but myself and nothing but my belly.*

Would that the misbegotten tooth puller were here now, Will thought. The man would produce beef ribs and ale for Will or suffer dire consequences. Shameful! It was shameful of the man to cheat a hungry boy who was good enough to assist him in cheating villagers. Will punched the empty air a time or two.

The rain started again as he began to walk up the deserted road. In the distance was a cottage, its window lighted by a candle. As a child he had often lingered outside such a cottage while day turned to evening and watched while men ate and women tended and children laughed and wrestled and shrieked.

Will sighed a gale of a sigh. It was likely warm inside that cottage and fragrant with new bread and stew simmering on the fire. He curled up beneath a tree and, supperless and wet, fell asleep.

FOUR

CONCERNING WILL'S ATTEMPTS TO

FILL HIS EMPTY BELLY

COME MORNING, Will started off on the road again, *scritch-scritch*ing at the start, but he found no pleasure in it this day. He was too hungry, too tired, too disheartened, and too alone. He was tired of apples and berries. He wanted the beef ribs the tooth puller had promised. He had not thought of such food until the tooth puller's offer, but now he wanted ribs and roasted chicken, fresh bread and cherry walnut cake. He wanted a fire of his own, a mug of ale, and a place to sleep out of the rain.

He kicked a stone along the road, hoping it would lead him to a town where he might pinch something to eat. Only a few kicks up the road, the stone skittered into a field and was gone. Will shook his head. Small things are so easy to lose, he thought: stones and apples and buttons. And hope.

Past stretches of woodland was a sunny meadow where sheep grazed. Sheep. Mutton stew, Will thought. And leg of lamb. With parsnips and onions, as they had it at the inn. In the home he had shared with his father they ate no lamb, no mutton, no beef, but only what Will could find or catch or steal—turnips and onions fallen from some farmer's cart, rabbits caught in snares of string, fish and frogs from the river, and an occasional chicken nipped from the neighborers. His belly rumbled at the remembering.

He walked through a field of purple and white flowers whose names he did not know and furiously beheaded them with a handy stick. Belike he should have stayed at the inn, where at least he ate somewhat regularly on what he could steal from the kitchen or pilfer from patrons, but then he remembered why he had run. Be a chimney sweep and cough his life away? He shuddered and kept walking, swinging the stick.

Off the road he saw a large house surrounded by a stone wall no taller than he, and up he scrambled. Below was a garden laced with paths, trees, rosebushes, and shrubs cut into fanciful shapes. A fountain spewed water into the air, where the sunshine turned the drops into rainbows.

Will studied the garden. Might there be such a thing as a cabbage growing in there? Or mayhap beans or greens or late-summer peas? He didn't see anything that looked fit to eat, but still his belly growled at the thought.

He stood atop the wall. Seeing no one around, he dropped to the ground within. The peaceful, herb-scented quiet was suddenly filled with furious barking and growling. Will froze. Dogs! Big dogs! He threw the stick in their direction and ran.

Growling and snarling, the dogs chased him up the path, past the shrubs, through the roses, and around the fountain. Finally he made for a tree and clambered up, scraping his legs and feet in the climb. "Go away!" he shouted down to the dogs, who jumped and snarled. "I hate you. I hate all hungry, hairy creatures!"

The dogs circled the tree, their teeth bared and glistening with drool. They did not look ready to depart anytime soon, so Will made himself more comfortable and examined his perch. Plums! He had climbed a tree heavy with plums, plump and purple and inviting. He chose one and bit into it. The sweet, soft flesh filled his mouth, and juice warmed by the sun ran down his chin. He found and ate the ripest fruit and threw the unripe at the dogs, muttering, "Choke on these, you nasty things."

"Brutus, Arthur, Ambrose, come," someone unseen called, someone with a light, musical voice, and the dogs stopped snarling and bounded away.

Nay, Will noted, peering from his perch—one of them still sat at the base of the tree, looking up into the branches and growling.

"Arthur!" the voice called again.

Arthur? The beast was named for the great warrior king who fought the Saxons? Will dropped an especially large green plum on Arthur's head.

"Arthur! Come!"

Finally Arthur stood. He lifted his leg and spewed a torrent against the trunk of the tree, shook himself, and bounded off.

Will sat in the tree for a while longer. His belly ached. Too many plums? Too much fear? Finally he climbed down, slowly, for his legs were sore and stiff. He found an easy foothold on the wall and over he went, finding himself away from the road on the farther side of the manor. Where he was he did not know, so which way he turned made no difference. He walked on.

He walked through fields where wheat swayed in the breeze and folk harvested the crops with great curved scythes and wooden rakes, hurrying to get the grain in before the rains came again. Crows hovered over hay-laden wagons and squabbled over the leavings in the fields. Will took great breaths sweet with the smell of new-cut hay.

At last he came upon a cluster of half-timbered cottages with roofs of thatch, where women sat at their looms in the sun or spun by the hedgerows. They looked at him with suspicious eyes, and he imagined how he appeared, with plum leaves in his hair, a torn dirty shirt, and a face that had not seen water in many a day. He washed his face in a puddle, found a clean shirt in the laundry some goodwife had draped over a holly bush to dry, and smoothed his hair down. He would attract less attention, he thought, if he did not look like a penniless vagabond. Although in sooth he was penniless and a vagabond. Nonetheless he squared his shoulders as he walked on.

Soon the cottages became more numerous, and Will saw ahead what might be an inn of soft cream plaster and timbers graying with age. He hurried closer. Aye, it was an inn. Over the entry late-summer roses grew, and the air was fragrant with lavender and other strewing herbs. A painted sign hanging over the door proclaimed THE LION AND THE MOUSE. He would sup this day. His belly rumbled enthusiastically.

Will went first to the stables. At the inn he had run from, he had tended the visitors' horses. He had also searched their saddlebags for anything of value to nip. The innkeeper always took what Will found, but the boy had managed to keep back a few coins, which he hid under a floorboard in the larder. Due to the abrupt manner of his leaving, he had abandoned the coins, and he mourned them now. He could have bought a sausage or a bit of chicken or a mug of cool ale.

There were horses in the stables but also a burly stable hand, so Will only nodded to the man and backed away. In the inn yard, at a trestle table under a tree, sat a group of ruffed and booted young lordlings, boisterous and roistering. Suddenly they leapt up and ran toward him. Startled, Will turned to flee, but the young men ran right past him, shouting, "Race! Race! We must have a footrace!"

As they ran, they pulled off their hats and caps, doublets and jerkins, and threw them down on the grass near where Will stood. Off they went, cheering and jeering, calling to each other, "Out of my way, ye fly-bitten ruffians!" and "By heaven, I shall run ye into the next county!" and leaving a cloud of dust behind them. Pickled like onions they were, Will thought.

He scuttled over to inspect their table. Not a crust of bread nor a crumb of cheese, and the wine cups were drained. They had eaten and drunk everything, the greedy pigs.

The lordlings had not yet turned back for the inn, so Will examined the piles of clothing they had discarded. He plucked out a fine brown leather jerkin and a cap of chestnut wool. *For when the nights grow cold,* he thought. He pulled the cap over his head and shrugged into the jerkin, which reached his knees. Swaggering a bit in all his finery, he left the inn yard and turned up a road, hoping the lordlings would travel the other way, especially the fellows now without jerkin and cap.

"You, boy, look like a sausage in too much bun," said a passing merchant with a glance at Will in the jerkin. Will scowled. Except for his empty belly, he felt like one of the lordlings himself and not like a sausage at all. He stood taller, stretching his neck, trying to look bigger than he was.

FIVE

OF HOW WILL ACQUIRES A MAGIC EGG,

A PARTNER, AND A FULL BELLY AT LAST

THE ROAD was rutted and rough with holes, and Will, hungry and weary, trudged, trudged, trudged. He passed a gatehouse flanked by stone lions guarding a tree-lined path leading to a fine manor house. 'Twas, no doubt, where the lordlings had come from. In such a house they would not miss one lowly leather jerkin, he thought as he smoothed it over his belly.

Finally in the distance he saw the towers and spires of a minster, reaching like fingers into the sky. A minster meant a town! Surely in a town he could manage to find something to eat. Something juicy, freshly roasted, and still steaming.

The rhythm of his walking inspired a chant: *Pork*

and lamb and fat beef ribs. Cabbages, radishes, parsnips,
and figs. Peach pie, fresh ale, and bacon from pigs.

While Will walked and murmured, the road grew crowded. Might one of these folks be after him? His shoulders tensed, and his heart beat faster. But certes, he convinced himself, the innkeeper would not have followed him this far, and he was no one anyone else would want.

With Will on the road were the customary beggars in rags, vagrant families seeking new homes, and those rogues called counterfeit cranks and Abraham men, shamming injury for gain. Cloaked and kirtled women carried buckets of milk, and men hauled sacks of grain. Packhorses laden with hides, with canvas, with bolts of woolen cloth in scarlet, blue, and saffron, trotted past wagons heavy with barrels and churns and wooden spades.

A metalsmith, with cooking pots and warming pans tied onto his donkey, clanked next to Will. "What town be this?" Will asked him, raising his voice to be heard over the clanking. "And why are all these folk hastening there?"

"It be Peterborough. Or Scarborough," the metalsmith answered, "or mayhap Foxborough or Dogborough. 'Tis some borough, I believe. There be a market fair here, so 'tis where we go."

Will's village had held fairs at times on market days, none so big that folk would travel far for them, but still fairs, so Will well knew that fairs meant food. His belly rumbled. Food like pigeon pies and roasted larks, apple tarts and gingerbread, spice cake and almond cake and hard-boiled eggs. Food ripe for the nipping by a clever, hungry young thief.

"'Tis a fine fair, I hear," the metalsmith continued. "Three days long. Goods aplenty to buy for those with coins, and smells to smell for those without."

The air thrummed with the shouts of hawkers, the cries of children, the bawls and bleats and brays of livestock, as Will joined the throngs heading over a stone bridge to a field. His eyes opened as wide as dinner plates, and he danced a few steps there on the road. 'Twas a fine fair indeed! The field was crowded with booths and stalls, some as small as carts and others nearly cottages, made of poles and boards and painted canvas, roofed over with branches or thatching or left open to the sky—more stalls, he thought, even than . . . than . . . than the number of apples he had lost to Nell Liftpurse, the foul hag.

Will's nose twitched. He smelled something, something savory and rich. He sniffed deeply. Roasting pork, it was, and—he sniffed once more—garlic. There was nothing in the world he loved more than roast pork, although in truth he had smelled it more often than he had eaten it.

He followed his nose into the center of the fair, past poulterers waving chickens by their feet and women with bark baskets of turnips and cabbages, to a booth where a whole pig was roasting. The porker was brown and crispy, dripping garlic-scented juices as it turned on the spit. Will stood and sniffed great sniffs while he wondered how some of that pig might find its way into his belly.

"Show me your coins or move away, boy," said the man tending the spit. "You are breathing air better saved for those with money to spend."

"Breathing is free, rude sirrah," said Will, "and sniffing and smelling."

The man came nearer, waving his carving knife, so Will had to be satisfied with sticking out his tongue as he moved along.

Merchants were busily arranging their stalls, setting out their wares, calling and cajoling passersby. "See walkers of the rope," someone called, "in the west field near the church," and another, "Wondrous feats of archery and wrestling and fighting with cudgels, hard by the leather stalls," and a third, "*The Tragical Tale of King Richard*, with dancing and song, noonday at the priory." Drums beat, lutes and fiddles played, ballad singers sang, but Will's belly called louder than any of these.

Up and down the narrow dusty paths between stalls he walked, past sellers of butter and eggs and cheese, fish fresh from the river, red apples and yellow pears. Here were leather stalls with fine, silver-buckled belts and carved saddles next to glovers, makers of rope, and scriveners writing letters for those who could not or would not. There, of much more interest to Will, was a pastry merchant who called, "Come get your nice ginger-bread, your spice gingerbread. It will melt in your mouth and rumble in your insides!" At the thought, Will's belly growled loud enough to be heard by a fine lady stand-ing near him, and she giggled into her hand.

Somewhere, Will hoped, there was a baker with his eye on his oven and not on his wares. Or a fruitmonger looking the other way. Or a roaster of meats too busy roasting to watch for thieves. Will walked to and fro, here and there, lingered and loitered, but saw no likely opportunity to pinch something to eat.

At an ale stall he saw a fat man with a fat purse bob-bing from his belt. His attention was on his ale and his companions, not his purse.

Will watched him. Nell Liftpurse would have that purse in a minute. Could he? Certes his hands were as nimble as hers. He waggled his fingers a time or two and wished he had thought to ask her for some instruction. Edging up close to the man, Will waggled his fingers again. Then he leaned over and with his outstretched fingers touched, just touched, the purse.

Suddenly he was knocked forward and fell to the ground, the purse in his hand, as a flock of unruly geese bumped and butted and shoved their way to market. "What ho, ruffian!" said the fat gentleman, shouting to be heard over the honking geese. "You would steal my purse?" He put his foot on Will's back and pulled the purse from the boy's hand. "Bailiff! Bailiff! Here to me!"

Will's thoughts raced as he searched for the words that would save him. "Nay, nay, sir, I was but jostled by the passing geese and did reach out to grab something to steady myself, and the purse came loose into my hand."

"Nonsense," said the fat man, and the other drinkers murmured and nodded. "It could not have happened that way. I will have the bailiff and—" At that instant, the last in the line of geese blundered into the man. Reaching out to steady himself, he grabbed the pennant adorning the ale stall. The pennant came loose, the stall tipped and tottered, and the man fell, pinning Will to the ground beneath him. Mugs and tankards flew about like raindrops in a wind storm.

"You see, sir," said Will to the man atop him, "it could have happened just as I said."

The onlookers laughed and saluted the two with their mugs. "'Tis true, sir, 'tis true! Let him go."

As the ale seller set the stall to rights, the fat man struggled to his feet. Will stood, wiped his sweaty hands on his breeches, and stumbled into the crowd, slipping now and then in the droppings the geese had left behind.

Beside an ancient yew tree near the center of the fair, a crowd circled a tall, long-nosed man in a gown of shiny green fabric, white ruff, and black velvet cap with a feather. He had dark hair to his shoulders and a short pointed beard of brown shot with red. Will watched as he threw into the air a yellow scarf that disappeared when he snapped his fingers. A wizard? A conjurer?

"Come, gentlefolk, closer. Prepare to be astounded," the man said. "For the next illusion, I require an assistant." He surveyed the crowd clustered around him and then motioned to Will to come forward.

Will shook his head. *Not I,* he thought, remembering the tooth puller. Assisting him had gotten Will nothing but wasted time and a stitch in his side from running. But this man was waving an egg about in his long fingers. *Ah, something to eat, if it be real and not a magic egg.* Will's empty belly urged him forward.

"Examine this egg," said the conjurer. "Take it in your hand. Feel it, smell it. Be it a real egg? Genuine and ordinary?" Will inspected the egg. It was speckled and warm to the touch, brittle and odorless, shaped like an egg. Aye, Will would indeed say it was a real egg. He nodded to the conjurer and turned to go, clutching the egg.

"Nay, nay," said the man, grabbing Will by his sleeve. "Give it here to me."

Will looked longingly at the egg. 'Twould have made a fine supper. He sighed, and his belly rumbled as he handed the man the egg.

"Now, young master," said the conjurer, "join your fellows and watch in amazement." He waved his arm about and chanted, *"Hey fortuna, numquam credo, passe, passe, et flotatus, fugit, fugit, levitatus!"* The egg flew about in the air.

Will was overcome with wonder. The egg floated up and down, side to side, an ordinary egg behaving most extraordinarily. He remembered Doctor Munster, the supper cheat, saying, "Things are not always what they seem, boy," so Will watched closely. He walked up to and behind the conjurer but could not see the trick. Was it truly magic, then? And was the magic in the words? he wondered. In the egg? Or in the man?

Calling *"passe, passe"* once again, the conjurer made the egg disappear and then, motioning Will to him, pulled it out of the boy's ear. "Take it. An ordinary egg, is that not true?" Will took the egg, examined it, and nodded.

The magician passed his hat around, and, as Will watched, people dropped coins into it. *Go to!* thought Will. *I can do that.*

He paused to consider. If the conjurer caught him, would Will be punished by some magic spell? Would grass grow in his ears or his nose fall off? But if he could collect a capful of coins, he could buy a fine supper without the risky business of nipping purses or provisions.

His stomach growled again, and he took the chance. He moved to the other side of the crowd and, whipping the cap from his head, passed it around. Few coins fell into the cap.

Will watched the conjurer on the far side, smiling and laughing as he went among the folk. *Mayhap I should do that also,* he thought. Though he had had little experience of merriment, he smoothed back his hair and licked his lips. He grinned stiffly at each person and touched his forehead in salute, and before long he could hear the clinking of coins.

Ere he could sneak away with his ill-gotten riches, his sleeve was grabbed and his cap seized. "I believe those coins are mine, bold fellow," said the conjurer. "And the egg also."

Confronted by the magician's dark, hooded eyes, Will gulped but held tightly to the egg. "I have had naught to eat since early morn, and that were only plums," he said. "I be most hungry. Might you not use your magic to pull another egg from the air and let me eat this one?"

"Not magic, boy. Ne'er magic!" whispered the man. "Say not the word. Magic be a burning offense." His voice grew louder. "I am Tobias of Froggenhall, master of the sleight of hand, adept of legerdemain, prince of prestidigitation. Trickery and illusions, that is my trade. I merely do tricks." He pulled a handkerchief out of Will's ear and blew his nose in it. Then he threw it into the air, whereupon it disappeared. Will stared, open-mouthed with wonder.

The conjurer poured the coins from Will's cap into the purse at his own belt. "It appears you are more able than I at cajoling coins from folk," he said. He peered closely at Will. "It must be your simple, open face. You appear innocent, though I doubt not it is an illusion." He pulled Will's cap back onto the boy's head. "Come back tomorrow. Gather in as many coins again and there shall be one in it for you."

Will thought the man might be a master of legerdemain, but certes he was no mind reader. Why, Will knew himself to be a thief and a liar who would take off with the coins, given the chance, and not look back.

Tobias of Froggenhall narrowed his eyes. "I shall keep close watch on you, boy."

Faugh! He was a mind reader after all. "I shall be here, good sir," Will said. Then, recalling his decision to get coins first: "Might you give me that penny now, in case circumstances require that you leave the fair in a hurry?"

The man rubbed his hands together, reached out, and pulled a penny from the air. "Go and find something more fit to eat than a raw egg," he said, handing the coin to the boy and taking the egg. "And come back tomorrow when the sun is overhead."

Will bit the penny. He did not know exactly why, but it was something he had seen the innkeeper do. It tasted real to him. "I will return," he said, "but first I do look to know how you made that egg fly."

"As you be my partner, young master . . ." The man stopped and looked quizzically at Will.

"Will Sparrow," said Will.

"As you be my partner, Will Sparrow, I will tell you." The man produced the egg from his sleeve and held it aloft. "Here be the egg you examined, and here"—another egg appeared in his other hand—"be the egg that flew, blown empty and pulled about by a hair attached with candle wax."

"In truth?"

"You must see beyond what you see, not look where I bid you look," the conjurer said. He clapped his hands and both eggs disappeared. "Look behind the obvious and see what I do not want you to see." Will recalled how Nell had diverted him with her kindness while she stole his belongings. He nodded in understanding.

The boy left Master Tobias and hurried off to find some supper as the day dwindled into evening. What might be offered that would suit both his belly and his purse?

There were stalls aplenty laden with meat pies and wedges of cheese, soups and stews and sausages, currant buns, and apples dipped in honey, but they were well watched. He would have to spend his penny.

"Here to me, here to me," a baker called to Will. "I be High Steward to the Stomach and Purveyor of the Pastry. Come see what delicacies I have to satisfy and delight you." Will traded his coin for a half mug of perry and a raisin tart, and he ducked behind a nearby stall to eat.

His belly at last full of tart and perry, he sat on a wicker hamper and fell asleep, the sounds of the fair playing in his dreams like music. Nell Liftpurse was in the dream, pulling eggs from the air, and Master Tobias made Will's father disappear.

By and by a thud nearby startled his eyes open, and he saw in the growing darkness a shape looming. The thing drew closer, and Will peered at it. His heart stopped and then began to thump. 'Twas some sort of monster, hairy and misshapen, wrapped in a blue cloak! The monster lumbered toward him, but Will was backed up against a wagon with nowhere to run.

God save me from creatures that stalk the night, he prayed as he threw his mug at the fiend and, putting his head down, shoved his way past. He heard it howling behind him but did not stop. He ran through the crowds, dodging visitors and merchants and acrobats, dogs and donkeys and gaggles of robustious youngsters.

He stopped to catch his breath. To his surprise, people were still whooping and laughing, enjoying the wonders of the fair and seemingly unafraid of any bluecloaked monster. He lost himself in the crowd, feeling safe among numbers. A group of musicians played before the gingerbread stall, and Will curled up behind. He watched a long while but no one, human or creature, came near him, and soon he slept again, fitfully, beset by dreams of monsters and angry shopkeepers and his body tied like a cooking pot to a donkey.

Six

ENCOUNTERING ODDITIES

AND PRODIGIES AND VARIOUS

OBJECTS OF WONDER

T WAS A monster, in sooth," Will told the conjurer the
next day, "a hideous, hairy monster with eyes that
glowed red and teeth that dripped blood." Will shuddered to remember. "Ten foot tall it was, wrapped in a
blue cloak that could not disguise its monstrosity. And
it came at me with evil intent."

The magician pulled a pigeon from the air and put
it in a basket. "Belike you were dreaming, boy."

"Nay, sir, no dream but a true monster. Here at
the fair."

"I will keep watch for your monster," the man said
as he made the basket and the pigeon disappear. "You
go and convince the good folk hereabout to come and

witness my amazing feats of legerdemain. There shall be an extra penny in it for you."

Will cleared his throat and called to passersby, "See a conjurer. Watch an egg fly."

"Nay, not so!" said the conjurer with a pinch on Will's arm. "Tell them of my great feats of illusion and spectacles of conjuring. Lure them!" He shoved Will forward into the crowd.

Hungry again, Will walked the fair, peering over his shoulder and behind trees for monsters as he went, calling, as he had heard the fair vendors call, "Here to me, here to me. Come see the Lord of Legerdemain, the Prince of Prestidigitation. Witness spectacles of conjuring that will astound you and fill you with wonder. At the old yew tree near the cheesemonger."

When enough of a crowd had gathered around Tobias of Froggenhall, he began. He juggled scarves and produced cards from his empty hands. He hid balls beneath mugs, made them vanish, and then pulled them from people's ears and noses. He swallowed a handkerchief and found it in an egg, turned eggs into birds and birds into eggs, and threatened to make a screaming child disappear.

Will gaped at the extraordinary doings and had to be reminded by a pinch on his arm to pass his cap. He found that fawning and flattery yielded even more coins than a grin and a salute. He called merchants *your lordship* and young men *master* and gave everyone his best fresh-faced, innocent smile. "I thank you, young mistress," he said to an overdressed, overpainted, over-old woman, and she added another coin.

The conjurer nodded at the coins in Will's cap and handed him two pennies. "I have business in town but will be here tomorrow noonday. Come back and there shall be more coins for you."

Will nodded. Two pennies! He hurried to the gingerbread seller and bought a large piece of gingerbread, then to a foodmonger for cheese and a pear—and a handful of cherry comfits when the stall keeper wasn't looking.

He ate as he walked through the fair, inspecting the crowd—women in brightly colored kirtles or starched ruffs, men in smocks and wooden clogs or padded doublets and fine leather boots. Small, ragged children pushed through the crowds, pulling at people's clothes, begging "Someut to eat?" and "A penny, sir, a penny." *Pitiful, mewling weaklings,* Will thought. He himself would never end up so, sniveling and begging. He was bold and quick-witted and could care for himself. Why God had created the poor Will did not know, but he was grateful that he was not among them.

Wiping his now-empty hands on his breeches, he stopped to watch a rope dancer somersault on a rope and balance a sword on his nose. Wrestlers struggled in the nearby grass. A tumbler flipped and flew through hoops and over men's heads while ballad singers sang the newest news and the oldest stories.

Shouts and cheers came from behind the leather stalls, and a mysterious *thwack thwack thwack*. Will pushed his way through a small crowd to see what was worth cheering.

In a field, a man in red with feathered cap called, "You, goodmen, come test your skill! Prizes to the fastest archer and the most true. Can you hit the mark?"

Archers were drawing great wooden bows and loosing arrows at wooden casks set up as targets. Arrows were stabbed upright into the ground at each man's feet so he could pull and nock them quickly, then, pressing the whole weight of his body into the horns of his bow, let the arrow loose, *thwack*.

"Let me try," Will said to a big man with a long bow and a short neck.

"Aye, lad," the man said with a laugh, "in forty years or more, when you be as tall as this bow."

"Or even the arrow," said another.

Biting his lip, Will stood as tall as he could. "Shooting an arrow could not be so difficult if a lackwit like yourself can do it," he said to the man with the long bow. The man smiled, shrugged, and handed Will the bow.

The bow was taller than the boy, so he rested it on the ground. He took an arrow, nocked it into the bowstring, and pulled back the string. Nay, he *tried* to pull back the string. He struggled and strained, and then, pressing the weight of his body into the bow as he had seen the men do, he loosed the arrow. It fell useless at his feet, and the men watching burst into great hoots of laughter.

"Go home to your mam, brat," said the big man as he took the bow, "and come back when you're man sized." Turning to leave, the laughter ringing in his ears, Will knocked over the man's tankard of ale with a small kick.

"My ale! Watch yourself, boy."

Will stumbled and careened through the crowd of archers, kicking over ale mugs as he went. *Now 'tis my turn to laugh,* he thought, and as the men cursed at him and sorted out the mess, he walked away.

O woe and lackaday, he lamented—when would he be too tall for taunts and teasing? How could he make himself *grow*? He walked on, kicking at the dusty path and anything that got in his way.

"Oddities and prodigies of all sorts here are seen! Strange things from nature!"

The caller, standing before a painted canvas booth,

was a small boy. Smaller even than Will. But an oddly shaped boy, with short arms and legs and a massive head. Will went closer for a better look. The boy proved no boy at all but a man, wrinkled and bearded, with a nose like a turnip and great bushy eyebrows as yellow as his hair. Never had Will seen such a strange man. Or was he no man at all but instead a troll or an evil dwarf such as were used in tales to frighten children?

The man had a back wide and strong stuffed into a tattered brown doublet and thick and powerful legs in trunk hose of scarlet that bagged at the knees. "Behold true wonders and marvels for only a penny," he called in a voice both thin and rough. "One single penny."

Will stood and watched. Those coming and going into the canvas booth did not seem afeared of the little man. They stared at him, taunted him, mocked and generally bedeviled him, and while his face turned dark with anger, he said nothing and did nothing to lead Will to believe he was dangerous. Will went closer.

Finally the man addressed Will. "You, boy, there, come see the prodigies. Only a penny."

Will stared. "In sooth you must be the smallest, ugliest person in the world."

"And you, young sirrah, would be the rudest," the little man said. "Wish you to see the wonder room? Enter, if you have the coin and the courage." And then he shouted to others standing about, "Come and see the wonder room! Only one penny." Two gentlemen in fine doublets so padded and stuffed that they moved only with difficulty paid their pennies and then, escorting a woman between them, entered the booth.

Will was curious to discover just what oddities and prodigies and objects of wonder were. "I would enter, but I have but a ha'penny left," he said.

The little man frowned. "Ha'penny perhaps for a one-eyed man to enter. A penny for such as yourself with two."

Will turned away. There be other ways in besides a front gate, he knew. He dawdled near the entrance until he saw the three previous visitors hurry out, the woman with faltering steps and a handkerchief held to her nose. He skittered behind her skirts and in, as easy as eating beef pie.

Will was alone in a space a bit larger than a sleeping chamber at the inn, comfortable for perhaps ten people, if the women's skirts were not too wide. The booth was open to the midday sky, but clouds kept it dim and Will had to squint to see through the gloom. All was silence within, and there was a foul smell of things wretched and dead. From one wall hung an assortment of stuffed animals, preserved fish, antlers, and turtle shells. On the other side stood a long, rough sort of table, on which various bottles, bones, and specimens were arranged.

He lifted crocks of mysterious liquids, examined bones and teeth, and wondered at the origin of a massive skull. Some of the objects were accompanied by labels. Having had a year of dame school before a rude word and a lost hornbook drove him out, Will could read when necessary, so, slowly and without comprehending all the words, he was able to identify those.

There was the skeleton of an infant sea monster, taken alive, it was said, from waters near Africa. All eyeless skull and sharp little teeth, tiny wings, and a lizard-like tail. A true sea monster? In sooth? Will was astounded. According to the label, the infant, with an evil temper but a sweet and melodious voice, died shortly after capture.

Next to it was the skull of a unicorn. Although he had heard many stories of the creature, he had never yet seen one. It looked a bit like a one-horned goat, he concluded, before moving on to a giant radish from Wales, a two-headed lizard, a live three-legged chicken, and the head of a one-eyed pig in a glass vessel. Its eye appeared to follow Will as he walked about the booth, and he shivered.

In a large, two-handled glass flask at the very end of the table floated a small creature, all bone but for a fishy tail and hair the color of sea grass that flowed and fluttered about. A baby mermaid, said the tag, captured off the coast of Ireland and now pickled like a cowcumber in brine. Will shook his head in amazement. This truly was a wonder room—sea monsters and unicorns and mermaids. He had never thought to behold such things in his life.

All agog, he proceeded to a small raised platform at the front of the booth. Someone sat there. As he approached, the person turned to look at him. Will froze. It was the monster, and it bellowed at the sight of him!

Heart pounding, he ran from the booth and through the fair. He did not stop running until a stitch in his side forced him to the ground, where he lay panting in the grass near a cap maker's stall.

It was truly a monster, and no dream at all, just as he had told the conjurer. What was it doing at the fair? Was he in danger? Or was—

Suddenly the air was filled with the sounds of terrible squealing and snorting, and Will was overrun by a huge, hairy thing. Bodikins! The monster had followed him! He struggled to get up, but the thing, snuffling and grunting, held him to the ground. He pounded and punched at it.

"Duchess! Leave it, Duchess! Sit, Duchess!" someone shouted loudly, and it must have been very loud,

Will thought later, to be heard over the beast's snarling and his own angry cries.

The beast ceased assaulting Will long enough for him to roll away and stand up, his back against the stall. It grunted at him again. And snorted. And oinked.

Oinked?

Will blinked. A pig. This beast was a pig, a big, long-legged, bristle-backed, ginger-haired, two-tusked pig with what Will would swear was a smile on its snout. "Whose pig is this? Call her off!" Will cried.

A round, red-faced man puffed up to them, still crying, "Sit, Duchess, sit."

The pig, at last, sat.

"Pah, boy, be not afeared of this impolite porker," the man said, gasping from his run. "She was merely searching your clothing for aught to eat. 'Tis part of our act."

"If I had aught to eat, I would have eaten it," said Will. He stood up straighter and added, "And I was ne'er afeared."

"Nay, certes not." The man flopped down next to the pig and began to scratch her ears. "This is the duchess, the Porcine Duchess, the world's smartest pig. She plays games with cards, counts, and tells you the hour of the day, to the wonder of folk everywhere. And I am teaching her to speak French." The man poked the pig in her bristly rear, whereupon the animal squeaked,

"Whee, whee," and the man laughed and hugged her tightly around her neck.

Will looked blankly at the man and the pig.

"Whee," the man said. "Like *oui*, French, you know? 'Tis a jest."

Will shook his head.

"No matter," said the man with a great gust of ale-scented breath. He threw his arms around the pig's neck and began to croon, searching for the right notes, "In Scarlet Town, where I was born, there was a fair maid dwellin' . . ."

Will frowned at the caterwauling and turned to leave.

The tuneless singing stopped. "Nay, young sir, do not go," said the man as he pulled at Will's breeches. "Come sit and speak with the Duchess. A fine specimen of porkhood she is, intelligent and noble. Why, one hour with the Duchess and you will come to prize pigs as I do. Trust me."

Trust him? Will trusted no one—not the mother who had left him, the father who had sold him, the innkeeper who had bought him. He did not trust the tooth puller or Nell Liftpurse, and he had been proved right. He did not trust Tobias of Froggenhall, although the man called him partner; Master Froggenhall was, after all, in the business of trickery. He was not going to trust this strange, ale-sodden man who preferred pigs to people.

The man pulled apples from a pocket, one of which he tossed at the Duchess and another to Will.

An apple? "What want you for this?" Will asked as he caught it.

"Want? Nay, nothing. 'Tis for you."

Will examined the apple and the man. Could it be there was no trick behind this, no price to be paid? Such was not his experience, but the apple was firm and smelled tart and sweet, so while the Duchess crunched and snorted through her apple, Will finally bit into his. He nodded his thanks to the man, who winked.

A pair of butterflies fluttered past Will's face and away. The Duchess rose to her feet and capered after the butterflies, her ears twitching and tail twirling.

Will watched her for a moment and laughed, only a small bark of a laugh but it astonished him, for he could not remember when last he had laughed.

SEVEN

GOBSMACKED BY

A PIG AND A MONSTER

DAY TURNED into dark, and Will found shelter beneath a tree in the heart of the fair, where he slept the night away. He surprised himself by dreaming not of monsters but of butterflies and woke in the morning somewhat lighter in spirit and very hungry. The sky was bright, and birds tweeted enthusiastically. He found it hard to believe in monsters on such a day.

A baker, putting out trays of warm bread, called "Good morrow" to the boy, who stumbled, putting a hand on the baker's stall to steady himself.

"A pox on you, clumsy boy," said the baker. "Have a care for my stall."

Will nodded his head in apology and hurried away,

one loaf tucked carefully beneath his shirt. He strode off between the stalls, chewing and calling to those visitors come early, "Gentle folk, see spectacles of conjury that will amaze and astound you! At the old yew near the cheesemonger. At the stroke of high noon." Now and then he looked over his shoulder for any monstrous entities or angry bakers but, seeing neither, continued on his way. "The marvelous and astonishing Tobias of Froggenhall will leave you gasping in wonderment. Noonday, at the old yew tree!"

Noon found him at the yew with Master Froggenhall and a crowd of folk prepared to be astonished. Will aided the conjurer with his tricks and passed the hat at the end.

He emptied the coins from his cap into the man's hand. The conjurer narrowed his eyes. Will reluctantly added several more coins. The conjurer raised one eyebrow, and another coin clinked into his hand. Satisfied at last that he was not being cheated, Master Froggenhall returned two pennies to Will, who now had four pence, having already knotted tuppence into the hem of his shirt.

Will inspected the stalls, stopping now and then to pick thorns and thistles from his bare feet. Boots. He needed boots, or shoes, but, alas, his few pennies would not provide them. He did buy a small leather purse to tie to his breeches and keep safe his newly acquired riches. Then his thoughts turned to food.

With pence in his purse, he decided not to risk nipping anything more. He sniffed a little and thought a lot and finally bought a currant cake, a hunk of strong yellow cheese, and the smallest mug of watery small beer. While he ate, he examined the toy stall: the drums, dolls and popguns, hobbyhorses and kites. He rued being too old for a childish hobbyhorse, for he might otherwise imagine himself a great warrior, riding his noble steed against the wicked Irish.

He was still gawking when familiar oinking and grunting announced the man with the pig. The pig must have been bathed and powdered, Will thought, for she smelled like new grass and lavender. She whirled her tail when she saw him.

"The Duchess be right pleased to see you, young sir," the man said, and the pig's tail went round and round.

Will finished his feast, belched in contentment, and, curious, followed the man and the pig to the edge of the fair.

"Good sirs and ladies," the man called to a gathering crowd as he climbed up on a tree stump, "I be Samuel Knobby." He touched his cap in salutation. "Knobby is my name, not my nature. For that I would be Samuel

Plump. Or Samuel Lardy." He laughed, and an ale-scented breeze stirred Will's hair. "Behold the Porcine Duchess, the world's smartest pig. She will awe, amaze, and astonish you. Come closer."

When enough folk had gathered, he climbed down and laid out a line of playing cards. Pointing to a girl with dark ringlets, he said, "You, little mistress, name a card."

The girl looked up at a nearby woman, who nodded permission. "The king of hearts," the girl said.

"Certes, the king of hearts!" repeated Samuel Knobby, and he turned to the Duchess. "Duchess, find the king of hearts for the wee damsel." The pig walked back and forth along the row of cards. Samuel Knobby sneezed—*ka-choo!* The Duchess stopped and pawed at a card. Everyone craned to see it. The king of hearts! Will was astounded.

Then, using the cards, the Duchess added numbers and successfully spelled out a merchant's name. She was rewarded with apple slices, which she ate greedily. Will allowed that the Duchess was right smart for a pig. Samuel, however, was likely coming down with an ague, for he sniffed and sneezed—*ka-choo!*—and coughed throughout the Duchess's exhibition.

"Finally," Samuel Knobby said to his awestruck audience, "the Duchess will perform a feat never before accomplished by a swine. Earlier I gave a penny to a young gentleman afore me here. The coin since has been passed from person to person until it has come to rest in someone's purse. I do not know which person or which purse, but the Duchess will find it." He patted the pig's head and gave her tail a friendly tweak. "Now go, Duchess, find the coin."

Huffing and snorting, the Duchess pushed her way into the crowd. She trudged around and through, grunting and snuffling at people's clothing, until she stopped before a lad in a blue apprentice cap. She snorted once more and then began to nose at the purse at his waist. The boy, laughing, opened his purse and produced the coin.

There were then a great many *ooh*s and *heigh-ho*s and *huzza*s. Samuel passed his cap around, and Will could hear the coins clinking into it.

When the crowd had moved on to other delights, Will followed the man and the pig to a nearby ale seller. "Master Knobby, I am gobsmacked," Will said. "I misdoubt the Duchess, no matter how smart for a pig, can truly read and spell and do sums. How did you make it seem so?"

"I cannot reveal my secrets, boy," Samuel said with a wink and a swallow from a brimming mug of ale, "but I will tell you that pigs have excellent hearing, and I do not have an ague."

Will nodded in understanding. "And how did she find the boy with the coin?"

"Ere we began, I rubbed the coin with mint, and the Duchess smelled it. Pigs is remarkable creatures, and the Duchess is the most remarkable." Samuel Knobby took another swallow. He saluted Will, called to the Duchess, and left.

Will watched Samuel Knobby walk away, a little unsteadily, followed by the pig. They were in sooth a comical sight, attracting a group of boys who trailed behind them, oinking and snorting and pulling the pig's tail. The Duchess squealed in fright. "Go away! Avaunt, you fiends! Leave off assaulting my pig!" Samuel Knobby roared, lunging at them. He picked up stones and, swearing, threw them at the boys, who dodged and scattered, oinking even louder.

Will stayed where he was, wary of putting himself in the way of being assaulted too. In sooth he cared for no one but himself and nothing but his belly, did he not? And perhaps boots. And currant cake. Still he was relieved when the boys left off abusing the pig and found a group of young women in ruffs and satins to annoy.

The whole spectacle moved on, and Will started back toward the oddities booth. He had one penny and a great deal of curiosity, and he planned to spend them on discovering just who or what that monster was.

The little man, his doublet ripped and cheek bruised, was again in front of the booth, cajoling fairgoers. "Come and see wonders of nature," he called. "Dragons and sea serpents and monstrous vegetables. Come and see. A theater of marvels. Only a penny. One single penny." The man did not, Will noted, mention the monster. Why not?

The man saw Will and said, "How now, puny stripling? So you are come back. Do you wish to behold the somewhat tawdry wonders within? Only a penny."

"Ha'penny if I vow to look with but one eye?" asked Will with a grin.

The little man frowned. "A penny, I said, and a penny it be. Now deliver a penny or be on your way."

Will flung the penny—his last—at the little man, who caught it and sneered, showing little brown teeth. "Go you in, then, if you bethink yourself braver than you were last time."

Will entered the booth. The sun was so bright overhead that it vanquished some of the nastiness and gloom within. While other folk were *ooh*ing and *aah*ing over the oddities, Will looked at nothing but the platform where the monster sat.

As he crept close, a shaft of sunshine illuminated its face. Out upon it! It was not the face of a monster he beheld, but that of a cat, a ginger-haired and sad-faced cat.

The creature was entirely hairy on its face, except

for its eyes and lips. It wore a dress, patched and faded, so Will guessed it was a she creature. She was nearly as tall as he, but he could not tell how young or old. A lettered sign on the platform announced she was the fearful Greymalkin, half wild cat and half human.

Visitors giggled or shrieked or turned away in horror, but the creature merely sat there, eyes on her lap, while the three-legged chicken pecked at her shoes. One young fellow crept close enough to pull on her sleeve. "Boo!" she snapped at him, and folks laughed as he hurried away in fright.

She turned her head toward Will. "You here again?" she asked him in a voice surprisingly sweet-sounding and soft. "Have you come to throw another mug? I still have the bump from our first meeting."

"You speak!" the astonished Will said.

"Aye. I speak, and I shriek, and I eat little boys for my supper. I am a fierce and wild creature with sharp teeth and claws, so go, shoo, run away in fear," she replied, but she said it with such sadness and self-mockery that Will did not think to be frightened.

He went closer. The hair on her face was reddish, fine, and silky, and her eyes were green as grass. She was mayhap a little younger than he. Ten years, belike, to his twelve or more. "The sign says you are half wild cat," he said to her. "Be that the truth?"

"Faugh! I am no part cat. 'Tis but Master Tidball's invention." She smoothed the wrinkles from her skirt. "Now that you have seen me and been horrified by my ugliness, you may leave. There lies your way," she said, gesturing with her chin. "Go! Avaunt! Aroint!" She turned her face away. Will walked from one side of the booth to the other, gazing at the creature and watching on-lookers respond with amusement or wonder or disgust.

When he and the creature were alone in the booth, he said to her, "I believe it is a trick of some sort. You have hair pasted on your face."

The girl narrowed her green eyes. "Aye, in sooth 'tis a trick, God's trick, and I am the butt of the jest." She stuck out her tongue.

A monster would not do that, Will thought, *nor a cat.* He paced the booth again, looking and thinking, and then said, "A shape shifter. Belike you are a shape shifter, from human to cat and back again. Aye, a shape shifter."

"And you are a foolish boy," she said.

"Can you purr?" Will asked.

"Go away," she said, and she lifted the chicken to her lap.

Will went.

EIGHT

IN WHICH WILL IS DISPLACED,

RESTORED, AND ON THE ROAD AGAIN

NOONTIME NEXT, the conjurer was not at the yew tree. Where was he? Will asked the cheesemonger and the pastry seller, the fire eater, a tumbler, and a purveyor of gloves, pins, combs, and laces. No one had an answer.

Will sat down and leaned against the tree, wondering what to do. His purse was empty again. The fair had ended. Folks were taking down stalls and packing up goods. Everywhere were horses and donkeys, wagons and carts and wheelbarrows, noise and dust. Where was the conjurer? Certes he had not gone away. The man had called Will partner. He would not leave a partner behind, would he?

"Be you Will Sparrow?" a voice asked. Will looked

up. "Froggenhall told me I would likely find you here." The speaker was tall, bald of head, and broad of shoulder, with bulging eyes of clearest blue in a friendly, moon-round face. He had greasy bits stuck in his beard, and he leaned on a stout walking stick.

"Master Tobias?" Will asked. "Where is he?"

"Gone to London for Bartlemas Fair," the stranger said. "Ere he went, he left you to me."

Left me? Will jumped to his feet. Was this the carter sent by the innkeeper? Or perhaps a merchant who trafficked in slaves for privateers? Just who the man was or what he wanted Will did not know, and he did not tarry to find out. Before another word was said, he was racing through the fair, on the run once again from those who would buy or sell or give him like a cabbage or a loaf of bread.

Will dashed between stalls and behind trees to the far end of the fair, where, having outrun the stranger, he stopped to catch his breath. His heart hammered, his shoulders slumped, and his belly heaved. Will thought himself many years too old for tears, but still his eyes prickled. He frowned and kicked at the dusty ground. Gone? Master Tobias gone? Will had grown accustomed to the work and the pennies and being a partner. Now he was alone again. What was he to do?

"You there!" someone shouted. "You, boy, in my second-best jerkin."

Will turned to look at the tall, red-haired youth. Jerkin? No doubt he was one of the young racers from the inn, the Devil take him!

"Bailiff!" the young man cried, grabbing Will by the sleeve. "Bailiff! I have caught me a thief!"

Will twisted out of the young man's grasp and ran off. He now had two pursuers to avoid. Where to go? And how to get there? He stripped off the telltale jerkin, tucked it under his arm, and ducked behind an ale stall to rest and to think. He sat for long minutes, catching his breath, although the odor of spoiled ale and stale wine made his belly tumble.

"A mug, if you please, Rob," a friendly voice said. "I am about thirsty work." Will peeked from his hiding place. It was the bald-headed man with the walking stick.

The man emptied the mug and reached it out to be filled again. "Know you of a likely fellow for hire? I seek someone to drive my wagon and assist me in sundry duties. Since my accident, I am useless and helpless." Will now observed wrappings around the man's right arm and ankle.

He bethought himself a moment. It could be the

man was not a villain but merely in need of assistance, just as he said. Will peered at him. He was a respectable-looking man, with a good-humored face and an easy smile. Will had learned well to be wary—but just then the red-haired young man passed by, scanning the crowd and mumbling about bailiffs and jerkins, and Will made a decision.

As soon as the young man was gone from sight, Will stood. "Sir," he said to the man with the walking stick, "the conjurer could not leave me to you, for I do not belong to him or anyone. But I wish to go from this fair, and if you be traveling on, belike I would go with you and be of service."

The man emptied his mug and wiped his mouth before he looked at Will. "A wagon accident ended with this fractured arm and twisted ankle. I seek someone to carry, to lift, to drive the wagon. Froggenhall said you were thieving, disrespectful, and cunning but would likely do."

He did? The conjurer, his partner, said that? It were true, Will knew, but it was downright unmannerly of Master Froggenhall to say so.

"I will give you tuppence a day and dinner," the man continued.

Dinner. And two pennies. Will nodded. "Done," he said.

The man examined Will. "But mayhap . . . I require . . . you may be too small to . . ."

Will's belly clenched at the thought of losing the pence and the dinner. "I can do it, sir. I am bigger than I look."

The man snorted in laughter. "Done," he said.

With memories of the tooth puller and the lost beef ribs haunting him, Will said, "I would, sir, have the first two pennies now, lest—"

"Do not trouble yourself, my boy. You shall ever have a day's wage for a day's work, but here is a penny now, on account."

Will searched the man's clear blue eyes and friendly face for signs of guile. Finding none, the boy took the penny and nodded. "Go we to London?"

"Nay. We are not ready for Bartlemas, but someday . . ." His face lit like a lantern. "Someday we will see Bartlemas Fair and it will see us. For now a small fair at Stamford not two days hence." The man leaned on his walking stick and touched his hat in salute. "I be Thomas Tidball." Tidball? Where had Will heard that name before? "We leave when the booth and its contents are packed in the wagon. Follow me."

Will peeked out from behind the ale stall and, not seeing the red-haired youth, followed Thomas Tidball as he hobbled away. Why had the man sought him? Will wondered. There were likely plenty of fellows stronger and more able who would be eager for tuppence a day and dinner. Fellows who were not called thieving and disrespectful. Why had Tidball engaged him?

The man stopped in front of a familiar painted canvas booth. The prodigies and oddities! This Tidball was the monstermonger! Belike that was why he had to settle for the assistance of a puny boy. The man traveled with monsters! Well, not monsters, but a very strange and hairy creature, an evil-tempered little man, a one-eyed pig, and a three-legged chicken. And pots, bottles, and baskets of ghastly things. Will shivered. Did he truly wish to be a part of this? He weighed his reluctance against his appetite and, thinking of the tuppence and dinner each day, followed the man into the booth.

The little man was inside, emptying the shelves of bottles and crocks and packing them into barrels and baskets. "This," said Thomas Tidball, "is Lancelot Fitzgeoffrey. 'Tis odd, is it not, an ill-tempered, ugly little man, a tavern brawler, with a name of such dainty elegance? Some call him Fitz, but I do not, preferring a more respectful form of address. Is that not true, Lancelot?" The man some called Fitz scowled, but Master Tidball smiled, and his good humor made Will feel easy.

Master Tidball's eyes searched the booth. "And somewhere is Greymalkin, wild cat and wild girl. Hiding, no doubt. She be somewhat shy and skittish." Will thought for his part the strange girl could remain hidden forever, if she wished. She was no monster, he knew, but her oddity made him uncomfortable, like a rash in a place he could not reach to scratch.

Tidball sat to rest his injured leg and directed Will to join Fitz in the packing of antlers, bones, and turtle shells. Before long the canvas booth had been emptied, dismantled, rolled, and fastened to the top of a roofed wagon. The baskets and barrels were stacked in the crowded interior, and the three-legged chicken tossed in.

"Fitzgeoffrey," Master Tidball said, "go seek the wild girl. We leave at once." And Will's heart thumped with apprehension.

NINE

ACCOMPANYING THE ODDITIES

WILL CLIMBED to the driver's seat and clucked to the horse, who was called Solomon, Master Tidball said with a smile, for his wise ways: "He eats anything, says nothing, and has never married." The wagon inched through the crowd of merchants and tinkers, jugglers and archers and alewives, on the move from this fair to the next.

Will was relieved to see that Tidball sat next to him on the wagon seat, and the oddities—including Fitz and the girl—traveled inside. They rode in silence through neat little villages with trees all around, their hillsides freckled with sheep. Fields stood empty, waiting to be sown with winter wheat. Golden leaves crunched under the horse's hooves, and Will could smell the coming autumn.

After a bit there came a furious knocking from inside the wagon, and Will pulled Solomon to a stop. Fitz jumped out. "I will walk a bit," he said. "I have a fancy to stretch my legs."

Will snorted.

"Did you hear something that amused you, stripling?" Fitz asked, raising one bushy eyebrow.

"'Tis but the thought of you stretching your legs. Belike you wish you truly could." He snorted again. "Stretch them."

Fitz frowned. "Fine words indeed from a wee, runtish fellow like yourself," he said, and he marched on ahead, pumping his arms and legs and muttering, "A flea, he is, a gnat, may beetles and bats swallow him!"

Will jumped to his feet, but Master Tidball pulled him down. "Pay him no mind," he told the boy. "He and Greymalkin are ever evil tempered, at odds with their peculiar gifts. If only they might accept that they are part of God's plan."

Master Tidball's reasonable words eased Will. He clucked to the horse, and the wagon started moving again. "God's plan?"

"Aye. God made them as they are for a purpose. To

amuse folk, belike, to liven their dull lives, to soothe their hunger for spectacle, to shock and frighten them so that they say, 'I may be but a poor farmer, but at least I am not a dwarf or a . . . a . . . whatever the girl is.'"

Will shrugged. God's plan, he thought. A mighty thing to know God's plan. How had Master Tidball come upon God's plan? Mayhap it was but Master Tidball's plan. Still, there must be some reason for their oddity. Were their monstrous outsides a warning to others that they were also monstrous inside? Will could believe it of the foul-featured, ill-natured Fitz.

As they rounded a curve, the air was filled with singing—merry and off-key and likely the result of too much ale at breakfast.

> In Scarlet Town, where I was born,
> There was a fair maid dwellin',
> Made every youth cry well-a-day!
> Her name was Barbra Allen.

Master Tidball, who had been nodding sleepily, woke with a start. "What is that caterwauling?"

"I believe 'tis singing," said Will, "and I believe I know the singer." A few more minutes of travel proved him right. "Good day, pig trainer," Will said, drawing up alongside the man pulling a handcart up the road, the

Duchess scrabbling at his side. "I bid you and the Duchess farewell. We are headed to Stamford fair."

"No need for fare-thee-wells, boy," Samuel Knobby said, "for we be moving on also. Fair to fair. We will see you in Stamford anon." He touched his cap and resumed his song:

All in the merry month of May,
When green buds they were swellin',
Young Jemmy Grove on his deathbed lay
For love o' Barbra Allen.

The singing grew fainter and fainter as Will drove the wagon onward.

Master Tidball began muttering to himself. "The Stamford fair be small. Could we draw twenty visitors each day? If we are credible and clever?" He shook his head and began muttering again. "Twenty-five. Nay, thirty. If we can but draw thirty visitors each day . . ."

Will computed silently: *Thirty visitors means thirty pennies. Two shillings sixpence. Tuppence for myself, the same for Fitz and the monster, leaves two shillings for Tidball. If he spends three pennies each on dinners for the three of us, that means fifteen pennies' profit. Oh, and hay for the horse—three pennies. That leaves twelve pence. A shilling. A whole shilling. A day. Every day.*

It seemed to Will that Master Tidball made a good living for someone who did nothing but watch others work. Will himself could do that, he thought. He could earn and keep that shilling a day, have a place in the world and plenty to eat. "How was it you first became master of oddities and prodigies?" Will asked the man when he ceased muttering.

"'Twas the infant mermaid," Master Tidball said. "I came upon her near Blackpool. Such a beauty, is she not? Folks paid a farthing to see her. Admire her fishy tail." Remembering, Tidball smiled. "I added more wonders and found that folks would pay more. So here I am, traveling the world with my odd little family, bringing joy to everyone in the world, or leastwise those with a penny to spare."

Early in the evening they came upon a stream with tall trees on either side. A soft breeze ruffled Will's hair and stirred the stream. "Here is where we stop," said Master Tidball, "here in this Eden."

They drank their fill from the stream and then sat back on the grassy bank. The creature was not there. Was she not thirsty? Will wondered. Did cats not drink?

Fitz carried a basket of apples, bread, and strong-smelling cheese from the wagon. "The girl Greymalkin," he said, "will eat inside." He gestured toward Will. "She be not fond of rude and saucy strangers."

"You, boy, come sit by me," Master Tidball said to Will, who did so. "The girl is lately testy and impossible to please," he went on. "Lancelot Fitzgeoffrey, you know I am right. Her acting the beast would make our fortunes. Half human and half cat! Imagine the crowds who would pay their pennies to see that!" Tidball passed an apple to Will, who took a large and noisy bite. "But of late," the man went on, "she will not pace nor growl nor roar, but only sits upon the stage and scowls. Talk to her, Lancelot, make her see reason."

"Not I," said Fitz. "'Tis you who wish her to play the beast. You talk to her." He dropped to the ground and glowered in silence, first at Tidball and then at Will.

I believe he is jealous to see me so friendly with the master, thought Will. He took another bite of the apple and spat the seeds near—but not too near—Fitz's small feet.

The night was clear and cool. Will pulled his—he thought it must now be considered his—jerkin on and curled to sleep near where Solomon was grazing, soothed by the familiar sound and smell of horse.

The morning dawned gray and shimmery with dew. Soon they were on the road once more. The company climbed gentle hills and passed great estates of gleaming stone manors and new grass, enclosures with puffs of sheep and specks of cattle, and vineyards heavy with grapes. The air grew heavy and damp, promising rain, and the wind blustered as they climbed toward a grove of limestone towers marking the city.

Stamford proved a town of shining white stone. The market square was crowded with stalls covered in thatch or canopies that fluttered and flapped in the wind. Will drove the wagon to a space between a seller of saddles and a church, and he and Fitz set up the booth and began to unload. The stuffed animals and turtle shells were hung inside, and the baskets of various oddities arranged. Will dusted off the unicorn skull and carefully placed the young sea monster. He and Fitz then carried the baby mermaid's flask into the booth.

By afternoon it was drizzling. People passed by quickly, their boots and the hems of their cloaks already bespotted with mud. Few stopped before the oddities booth, and none revealed a desire to enter.

"Faugh, but this is a poor fair," said Master Tidball, who sat on the low stone wall that surrounded the churchyard. He pulled his cloak closer around him and spat in the general direction of the ground. "Lancelot, ensnare me a visitor or two."

Fitz began: "Come and see! Oddities and prodigies of all sorts here are seen. A one-eyed pig and a three-legged chicken. Behold true wonders and marvels for only—"

"The girl," Tidball growled. "Tell them of the wild girl."

Fitz frowned but began to call, "For the satisfaction of the curious we offer here a girl of unusual qualities who discourses most eloquently—"

"No! Tell them of her wildness, her fearsomeness, her monstrosity!"

Fitz crossed his arms and said nothing.

"You miserable minnow! You may be small, but your ingratitude is immense. Go from my sight." He turned to Will. "You, boy, you do it."

Fitz backed up against the oddities booth and scowled as the boy tried to remember what he had done for the conjurer and how it might serve for the oddities. "Uhh," he began, his voice cracking and creaking as it had begun to do of late. He cleared his throat and began again. "Here to me, here to me, see astounding spectacles and unusual chickens and a monster, a sea monster, and a strange creature who might, uhh . . ."

Master Tidball groaned and muttered, "Useless, useless, useless," wobbled to his feet, and limped off.

"God's mercy, Hugh!" Will heard someone shout. "Look at that ugly boy." The speaker, a young ruffian, was pointing at Fitz.

"Nay, Alf," said his companion, a spindly boy with a face speckled with scars, " 'tis a dwarf, a black-hearted elf with mischief in his mind!" And both boys began to laugh.

Will barked a laugh of his own—Fitz was a black-hearted elf indeed—and the boys turned to look at him. "This be a sight I ne'er thought to see," Alf said, pointing at Will. "Another one! Two dwarfs, one uglier than the other!" Their laughter overtook them, and they stumbled about, pushing and shoving each other.

Me, a dwarf! Will stood as tall as he could, his face flaming. A rough, freckled hand came from behind him to rest gently on his shoulder. Samuel Knobby's voice said, "You, boys, do ye like riddles? For I have some fine new ones."

The boys stopped laughing and studied the gorbellied Samuel. "Hearken to me, Hugh," said Alf, "I too have a riddle." He gestured toward Samuel. "It is large and fleshy. Be it a man or a gourd?"

"I believe 'tis a melon," Hugh said, and, with a punch to Alf's arm, added, "Now, quiet. I wish to hear the riddles."

Samuel smiled, and Fitz moved closer. "Then tell me: If you bite me," he said, "I bite back. What am I?"

"A mad dog," said Hugh, and Samuel shook his head.

"A horse," said Alf. Samuel shook his head again and slapped his leg in merriment.

"A weasel?" Will guessed, his curiosity stronger than his anger.

"Nay," Samuel snorted through his laughter, "I know no one who would bite a weasel. 'Tis an onion," he said. "Now, here is a riddle boys do like: What is it that rich men wrap up and keep in their pockets but beggars throw away?"

The boys narrowed their eyes and chewed their lips in thought but had no guesses. Fitz was silent.

"Think on it, boys. Make use of your heads." No one answered. So, "'Tis the snot from their noses," Samuel said. His listeners snickered and sneered, and Will wiped his nose on his sleeve.

Duchess came then, snorting and grunting, from behind the oddities booth. "Ugly pig!" Alf cried, and "Stupid pig!" and Hugh repeated "Ugly stupid pig!" and threw a clod of mud at her.

"Hold your tongues, churlish pups," said Samuel Knobby. "Pigs be glorious creatures, smarter than people, more honest, more loyal, and a good deal more mannerly."

The boys laughed. "Nay, 'tis not true," Alf said. "Pigs is stupid."

"'Tis true indeed. Why, I have riddles the Duchess can answer faster than you."

"Nay," said Alf again.

"Aye," said Samuel. "Duchess, what is it that stands straight as a soldier and offers its head so we may eat?"

Alf shrugged, Will frowned, Hugh scratched his head, and Fitz looked down at the ground, but none had an answer. Samuel poked the pig in her rear, whereupon she squeaked, "Whee."

"True, indeed," said Samuel. "The answer is *wheat*."

"'Tis a trick, scurvy knave, a trick," Alf and Hugh cried, but Fitz and Will laughed.

"Nay, no trick, but to prove her wits, she shall do it again," said Samuel. "Duchess, how does a man make a river of salt?"

This time Fitz shrugged, Alf frowned, Will scratched his head, and Hugh looked down at the ground, but still none had an answer. The pig was poked again, and again she squealed, "Whee."

"Certes, 'tis true. *Weep*. To make a river of salt, a man does weep. You see, pigs do be smarter than people." He scratched the Duchess behind her ears. "Also clean, curious, and sensitive to scorn, so I pray you ne'er again speak of stupid pigs, pigheadedness, dirty pigs, fat as a pig, or any such." He drew a leather bottle from beneath his doublet and took a deep pull. "Pigs do take a bit of care, need to be kept cool and wet and their bellies full, but I ne'er saw a pig who teased and taunted another pig." Samuel winked at Will.

"Now, come and follow the Duchess here," Samuel continued, "who will perform at the west end of the square. Pigs must be kept busy lest they fret. And we shall astound you with what else she do know." The man and the pig left, followed by Alf and Hugh, who began again to push and shove each other as they followed, and Fitz.

TEN

OF AN ALARM GIVEN,

A NOSE BLOODIED, AND

HURTFUL WORDS SPOKEN

WILL SPARROW," cried Master Tidball, striding
back to the oddities booth, "I see the horse and wagon
here still! I do not fancy paying a fine to the keepers of
the fair. Hasten to take Solomon and the wagon to the
field yonder, and give a penny to the man who watches
the wagons." He sat down on the wall and stretched out
his bad leg.

A penny. Will had just the one Tidball had given
him and no more. He cleared his throat loudly. "Sir, I
have but one penny, on account for my wage. I believe
now would be a good time to give me—"

"Fitz is the man to see about wages," said Master
Tidball. He struggled to his feet again and called to a
passing man in tall boots and hooded cloak, "I have

wonders inside to astound and astonish." To Will he whispered, "Take the horse and wagon, boy, and go."

Will took Solomon and the wagon to the field nearby, where merchants and fairgoers had parked their vehicles. He gave his only penny to a man who promised the wagon would be safe and Solomon well tended. Coming back, he inspected the market stalls stocked with saddles and baskets and woolen cloth, plates and candlesticks of pewter and brass, heaps of apple tarts, creamy cheeses, and plums. His mouth watered. He would, he determined, find Fitz and collect his wages. Four pennies, by his reckoning, and mayhap tomorrow's two in advance. And another to replace the one he had just given away. Enough for cherry almond cake and pork ribs, small beer and walnuts, and something left.

The boy nearly stumbled over Fitz behind the leather-goods stall. The little man, face bruised and bloodied, was crouched on the ground, puking and spitting. The drunken sot had been brawling, Will thought. He had seen his father thus many an evening.

When Fitz sat back, Will began. "Fitz, I have come to obtain my wage."

"Go away, boy. Do not bother me." Fitz spat a bloody tooth onto the ground.

"I have labored these days honestly and honorably and require that you—"

Fitz stood. He spat out another glob of blood, narrowly missing Will's bare feet. "Goats and monkeys! Aroint you! Betake yourself! Do not trouble me about your pennies. I have no pennies, no shillings, no pounds. Go and bother someone else."

Will did not move, but Fitz staggered away. *The sodden-witted cur,* Will thought. *He has drunk away my wage and I am left with nothing! I will leave this company,* he decided, *but not before collecting the pennies owed me.*

As Will made his way back toward the oddities booth, his nose began to tickle. Smoke. He smelled smoke from somewhere. Fire was always a problem in a place of flimsy stalls and thatched roofs.

As he drew near the ale stall, the smell grew stronger. A lone man was leaning against the stall, his head wreathed in clouds of smoke. "Fire!" Will called. "The ale stall is on fire!" But no one heeded him. The stall would burn up, and likely the entire Stamford fair, Will thought, and he would never get his pennies. Will ran to the stall, grabbed a tankard, and dashed the contents about the stall and the man himself.

Beer streaming from his cheeks, the fellow removed a clay object from his mouth and grabbed Will by the arm. He shook the boy hard and shouted, "A pox on you, villain! You spoiled my shirt, wasted my beer, and soaked my pipe. Bailiff!" he cried. "Bailiff! I have caught me a vandal!"

"Nay, sir," Will said, squirming under the man's rough hand. "'Twas only that the stall was on fire . . . your very head was smoking!"

"Fool! Witless lout. I was but enjoying my pipe!" He wiped the beer from his face with the hem of his shirt before shaking Will again.

"Soft, Ned, soft," said a man newly arrived. "Belike the boy has never seen someone drinking smoke."

Drinking smoke? Will's forehead crimpled in confusion.

"'Tis sotweed," the newcomer explained, "tobacco from the colonies, set afire, and the smoke is breathed and swallowed. Some say there is nothing from the New World more valuable than this plant, a remedy for sores, wounds, infections of the throat and chest, and the plague." He loosed Will from the wet man's grasp and walked the fellow, dripping beer, away.

"Fire!" someone behind Will squeaked. "He thought the man afire and poured beer on his head!" And a gaggle of boys commenced squeaking and jumping about, calling, "Fire! He thought the man afire!"

"Alf, look, this fool is the boy dwarf from the oddities booth," hollered Hugh, for they were among the gaggle. "Do something odd, boy."

His blood a-boil after a day of insults, humiliations, and disappointments, Will threw himself at Alf, who was biggest but nearest, and shoved him a mighty shove before turning to run. But Alf was too quick, and Will had not gone more than a few paces before he was dragged down. At first Will saw only Alf's feet, but then the bigger boy was on him, all teeth and nostrils as he strewed punchés on Will's head. "Get off me, you beetle-headed clotpole!" Will shouted. "Fat-witted worm!" while the onlookers called, "Thrash him, Alf!" and "Crush him!" and "Bloody his nose for me!"

Of a sudden there was daylight and the cessation of pummeling as a growling someone thumped and walloped Will's tormenters. Will, facedown in the dirt, heard scrambling as the boys ran away. "Someone ought to teach you to fight, pup."

Fitz. He lifted Will by the back of his shirt.

"Who? You? What could you teach me, you runt? I have seen what fighting gains you—black eyes and broken teeth!" Will's arms swung futilely in the air. "Put me down, you puny, drunken measle! Drink-sodden botch of nature!"

Without a word, Fitz dropped him and strode away.

Will cursed as he spat dirt from his mouth, wiped blood from his face, and struggled to his feet. Fight? He was too small to fight—he knew it. Running and hiding.

He spat again. He was just the size for running and hiding.

The promised rain began. Wet, sore, and still angry, Will returned to the wagon, rolled underneath, and slept the afternoon away.

He woke to voices. "I am off to the Blue Bell in Ironmonger Street," said Master Tidball. "Do not trouble me unless someone truly is afire at the fair."

Will heard laughter, so he knew Fitz had told Tidball of the scene at the ale stall. But he was hungry, so he crawled out to see what might be had to eat.

The rain had stopped for the moment. Fitz and the creature were sitting by a small fire. She saw Will and, ducking her head, stood and took a step back toward the wagon. And stopped. She looked closely at Will. "You are not a stranger," she said, "but that pitiful boy from Peterborough fair. A stray Master Tidball has taken in. I be not afeared of you." She sat down again and stretched her legs toward the fire.

Will glared at her. "A boy, aye. Peterborough fair, aye. But not so pitiful as some," he said, jerking his head toward her. Then he sat down on the far side of the fire.

Fitz threw him a heel of bread, none too fresh, and a plum. "Here, churlish boy," he said, "fill your mouth with these in place of those ugly words. Would I could stitch your lips together to keep you silent."

"And I would stitch yours so you would not be able to drink my wages away, you muddy-mottled rascal," said Will.

Fitz snorted. "Fine words from a mewling wheyface such as yourself."

The rain began again. Fitz went to the booth to guard it, the creature Greymalkin crept back into the wagon, and Will crawled beneath. His belly churned with anger after such a day. Indeed, he would collect his pennies from someone, anyone, he decided, and be on his way.

ELEVEN

FETCHING A JUGGLER AND

FINDING HIM UNLIKELY BUT TRUE

THE MORNING brought rain again. The few fairgoers, huddled in their sodden cloaks, went about their
business quickly and did not stop to be astounded or
astonished. Will sat on the church porch, where the
overhang offered him some protection from the wet,
and watched.

Despite the weather, a passing family laughed
loudly, and Will turned to study them: a round-faced
woman and a round-bellied man with a child on his
shoulders, who shrieked with delight as he pulled on
the man's hair. Will watched them go. *Bah,* he thought,
*a pretty picture indeed, but belike she will leave, he will
drink, and the lad be sold for a climbing boy.* Will stood,
hitched up his breeches, and looked away. *Me,* he thought,

I care for no one but myself and nothing but my belly. And my wages. And staying dry.

As wet morning turned to misty afternoon, Samuel Knobby trundled by with his pig and his handcart. "The Duchess and I are for Ely, young Sparrow," he said, "where I trust there are more fairgoers and fewer raindrops."

"Indeed," said Master Tidball as he and Fitz appeared from the oddities booth. He mopped rain from his face and his bald head with his cap. "A fine fair, it is said, for horses, cheese, and hops. And for oddities, I hope." He laughed. "We also shall leave this place of rain and phantom visitors and make for Ely. Sparrow, you and Fitz pack the specimens and make them ready for travel. Fitz then will fetch Solomon and the wagon here and commence loading." Master Tidball nodded to Will. "And you, boy, will hie to the west end of the fair, hard by the inn yard, where you will find a juggler. Fetch him and meet us in the field near the east road. He will travel with us to the fair at Ely, and farther if he can be so persuaded."

Will and Fitz packed the oddities and gathered them near the churchyard. Then Will hurried to the inn, and indeed a juggler was there in the yard, entertaining those few folk reluctant to leave the fairgrounds even with the damp. The boy watched for a few minutes, eager to be amazed by the juggler's skill.

The man juggled colorful scarves that flew like brightly hued birds. He threw balls into the air and caught them in varied designs and patterns, but it did not seem to Will that the juggler was particularly able or adept. Though the crowd clapped and called "Huzzah," Will was not a bit amazed. At Peterborough fair he had seen a man juggle knives and flaming torches. Five, that man juggled *five* torches, even in the dark. They whooshed as they cut the air and gave off bits of flame like tiny shooting stars.

This juggler finished his tossing and catching, and he placed the balls and scarves in a canvas bag. "I am here, Master Juggler," Will said, "to escort you to Master Tidball's wagon."

"Well met, young sir," said the juggler, a tall, thin man with few teeth and leathery skin marked with pocks like a dusty road in a drizzle. "I am in readiness." He bent down, gathered up his coin-filled cap, and poured the coins into the pouch at the waist of his much-mended doublet. He shook droplets off the cap and put it on his head, threw the bag over his shoulder, and said, "My name be Benjamin Bassett. And you are?"

"Will Sparrow," he said, "partner to Tobias of

Froggenhall, master of the sleight—" and then he stopped, remembering that Master Tobias was gone and he himself was only Thomas Tidball–the–monstermonger's drudge.

Will and the juggler started up the path. "We turn to the left at the gingerbread stall," Will said before losing himself in thoughts of what sweets his forthcoming pennies would buy.

"Here, young Sparrow," called the juggler, "did you not say we turn at the gingerbread stall?"

Will had passed it by. He nodded sheepishly and turned back to the juggler and the right path.

"Be careful, *cave et cura*," the man said, pulling Will aside as a group of youngsters, splashing and sliding through the mud puddles, stumbled past them.

"Gramercy, sir juggler," Will said. "Leastwise one of us has his eyes open."

"*Auxilio ab alto*, with help from on high," said the juggler.

Will wondered what he meant, but they had reached the field where the wagon waited, booth rolled and stored on top. Benjamin and Fitz exchanged *How now*s and *Well met*s, and Fitz produced onions and sausages from a basket and a pail of ale. With their cloaks wrapped tightly about them, Fitz and Benjamin sat on the ground and leaned against the wagon to eat.

"Where is the, er, girl?" Will asked.

"In town with Tidball," the little man said, throwing a sausage to Will. "Foolish gentlefolk, the ninnies, pay dearly to sup with the Wild Girl, and that nip-cheese Tidball seizes every opportunity to fatten his purse." Fitz took a long pull on his mug, and he spat in the direction of the town. "He said we leave tomorrow at first light."

Will moved to chew his sausage away from the grumbling of the short, ugly man. Fitz might call Master Tidball a nip-cheese, but the master never failed to see to their bellies. *If Fitz thinks so little of Master Tidball, let Fitz return his sausage,* Will thought. How would it be, he wondered, to be trapped in such a body? It might account for the little man's ugly temper.

Benjamin Bassett left to relieve himself, and Fitz lay back, eyes closed. Will took the opportunity to examine the juggler's bag, on the lookout for coins or cake or anything worth nipping. Alas, there was nothing but balls and scarves and an extra pair of patched hose.

"Why does Master Tidball want this fellow?" he muttered to himself. "He is hardly a fine juggler and tosses and catches only scarves and balls. I have seen better."

"Ye wee want-wit, are ye too daft to notice?" Fitz asked without opening his eyes. "This juggler is blind."

Will shook his head. "Nay, he is not. He led me here

when I missed a turn; he warned me when I looked to be overrun by revelers. For cert he is not blind."

The returning Benjamin dropped down next to Fitz and saluted Will with a finger to his cap. "*Vero*, in truth he is," the juggler said, "but his nose and ears work exceedingly well."

Will was astounded. "A blind juggler? Is Master Tidball looking to assemble a mighty army of oddities?"

Benjamin shrugged. "What say you, Fitz? Why is he so eager to have me join you?"

"He has dreams of Bartlemas Fair in London," said Fitz, "and to that end seeks out the oddest of oddities and the most prodigious of prodigies."

"*Libertas inaestimabilis res est,* liberty is a thing beyond price, and I do not hurry to give mine away," said Benjamin with a shake of his head. He pulled a small wooden flute from his bag and began to tootle a tuneless tootle.

Will sat again and pondered. A man with a limp and a walking stick. A blind juggler. A bad-tempered, thieving dwarf. A creature half cat, half human. A one-eyed pig head and a mermaid baby. He shook his head again. In sooth he was the only sound one among them. He would stay with them long enough to get the money owed him, and then he would . . . he would . . . he did not know precisely what he would do, but he was no oddity.

Suddenly a mug flew through the air and shattered against the side of the wagon, splashing ale like raindrops. Will's heart gave a mighty thump. "Fie on Thomas Tidball!" Fitz shouted. "May his dreams be as empty as his heart, the mingy moldwarp!" He belched loudly. "There's no more honor to be found in him than in a cow turd, the loathsome, hellborn knave!"

A pox upon this Fitz, thought Will, whose heart still thumped, *the hateful man slandering a goodly fellow like Master Tidball! A pox upon him! Upon them all!* As soon as he got his money, he would go. He, too, belched and then asked, "Does Master Tidball know that you withhold my wages? When will you give me my pennies?"

"When there be a snowstorm in Hades," Fitz responded. He stood, kicked at the remains of his mug, and shouted, "To bed! We leave at first light and wait for no one."

Fitz and Benjamin slept under the wagon, but Will stayed outside by himself. It appeared Fitz would continue to drink up Will's wages. Will now had bread and meat from time to time and an occasional mug of ale, but he wanted more. He wanted to be dry and safe. He wanted food every day—nay, twice a day. And he wanted . . . he wanted . . . he did not rightly know. Finally he sighed, pulled his jerkin over his head, and pushed the wanting away.

TWELVE

ENCOUNTERING LATIN, THE FEN

COUNTRY, AND FRIGHTFUL

THINGS IN THE NIGHT

IN THE darkness Will could hear Benjamin grunting and tossing. Finally the man crawled out from beneath the wagon. "Can you not sleep on this hard ground, Master Juggler?" the boy asked.

"Nay, 'tis not the ground," said Benjamin, dropping down next to Will. "I am but fretting about what I shall henceforth do. Your Master Tidball offers food and transport, but Fitz is of the opinion that the man is a varlet."

"Fitz is an evil-tempered, ugly little man with nothing good to say of anyone. I have ne'er seen sign of bad temper or bad behavior in Master Tidball. In truth he is much more amiable and honest than Fitz himself," said Will.

"Nonetheless, as the ancients say, *beneficium accipere libertatem vendere est,* to accept a favor is to sell your freedom."

Will took his stolen jerkin and folded it to make a pillow for his head. "What are those strange words you say?"

"Latin, my boy, Latin, *lingua mater,* the language of churchmen and scholars, poets and the law. All the great works of God and man are written in Latin."

Will recalled how he long ago had learned to read English. Never could he have done it with his eyes closed. "How learned you Latin, you who are blind?"

"I was not blind *ab ovo,* from my beginnings, but a scrivener, copying wills and deeds for those who wanted copies. Until the pox found me."

Will thought of the man's deeply pitted skin and let out an *oof.*

"Aye, indeed, the scars. Lord Pox took my face and my sight and my pride. Ah, woe! I cowered near the wall of the city, bestraught, not caring what befell me, waiting to die."

"But you did not die."

"Nay. Rather *in articulo mortis,* at the point of death, I heard someone say, 'The pitiful worm. Why does he take up space in this world? He has no more use than a blind juggler.'" Benjamin's voice grew louder. "My blood ran hot, leapt in my veins, fired my heart. Who was he, this unknown rude man, to judge me and find me worthless? No longer would I study *ars moriendi,* the art of dying, I decided. I would live."

He would, said Benjamin, cease regretting the infirmities life had tossed at him and prove that unknown fellow wrong, and do it by being the very thing the man scorned—a blind juggler. "I was determined *aut vincere aut mori*—to succeed or die."

Will yawned.

"You are right, young Sparrow," Benjamin said. "*Satis verborum.* Enough words." And he settled down into the warmth of his cloak.

Will's body yearned to rest, but his head was spinning. How could someone decide to die or not to die? How did a blind man become a juggler? Would being blind be worse than being sold for a climbing boy? Finally he fell asleep, but his dreams were empty and cold.

At dawn Will got stiffly to his feet, rubbed his eyes, and stretched. The girl stood watching him. She and Tidball must have returned sometime in the night. He backed away but didn't run—she was but a girl, after all, even if she did look like, well, a cat. Though he was not afeared of girls or cats, he was distinctly uncomfortable with this creature who was neither one nor the other—or mayhap both at once.

In the growing light of morning, her fur was so light it nearly disappeared, and she seemed almost an ordinary girl in a dress of some stiff red stuff with a limp ruff around her neck. Greymalkin the cat, Tidball had called her. How did she eat? Like a cat lapping at spilled milk? And what did she eat? Mice? Or bread and ale as the rest of them did?

Will watched her as he chewed his bread. To his disappointment, he discovered that she ate like a girl, an ordinary girl, and wiped her face on her skirt, after which she looked at him with a glance that made Will believe she knew what he was thinking and stuck out her tongue.

"To Ely, my children, to Ely!" Master Tidball shouted, and the company made ready to go.

"Good morrow, Solomon," Will whispered as he hitched the horse to the wagon. He stroked Solomon's nose a time or two before climbing into the driver's seat.

Fitz and Benjamin strode ahead of the wagon, the girl rode inside, and Master Tidball took the seat next to Will. The troupe was on the road once more, east to Ely.

A fine, fair morning it was, with the air fresh washed by the rain. The landscape was soft, green and yellow and red with the coming autumn, and the road was lined with farms and pubs and inns for travelers.

The wagon wheels threw up stones and pebbles as they drew near Fitz and Benjamin, and Fitz scrambled and scampered out of the way, cursing the wagon and the driver. Master Tidball laughed and began to sing:

> As I went out to take a walk,
> Between the water and the wall,
> There I met with a wee wee man,
> The weest that ere I saw.

"Sing with me, boy," Master Tidball said, and Will did so, for he had learned the song at the inn:

> Thick and short was his legs,
> And small and thin his knee,
> Between his eyes a flea might go,
> And between his shoulders, inches three.

Fitz glowered at them as they passed. "That is Lancelot, to the life," Tidball said, and he doubled over with laughter. "Oh me," he added, catching his breath, "oh me, he does make me laugh, the ugly, disagreeable little clown."

"Is that why you put up with his arguments and

his bad temper?" Will asked. "Because he makes you laugh?"

"Aye. And because I thought to show them together—the wild girl and her tiny overseer. 'Twould have been a sight to see. Once she did as I bade her, but now she won't, and if she won't, he won't." Tidball smacked his knee and grumbled, "Sea-monster skeletons and three-legged chickens are not attraction enough. I must have something spectacular: a dog-faced man, perhaps, or a giant, or an armless man who plays on a lute with his feet."

He pulled a tattered piece of paper from his sleeve. "See this, young Sparrow—I have spent many years searching for such as this."

Will looked. It was a broadside with a drawing of two infants—no, one infant—no, perhaps one infant with two heads? He peered closer. No, it was two infants, joined together at the belly. He shuddered. Could such a thing be so?

"Monstrous children." Tidball sighed. "Delightful! If I could but find such as these, it would make my reputation and my fortune. And then Bartlemas Fair! I would have something extraordinary to show at Bartlemas Fair."

Will looked at the picture once more before Tidball folded it and tucked it back in his sleeve. Were there really such monsters? What did it mean? Evil? Witch-craft? What became of poor babes such as these? In heaven were they still one, or could God make them two? And if he could, then why had he made them one at all?

By afternoon there were fewer villages and fewer trees as they found themselves in the fenlands. Will marveled at the sights, so different from the gentle hills and fields they had left. The low-lying flatlands pocked with misty marshes and mires of reeds and rushes were flecked with windmills and crisscrossed by dikes and drainage ditches. In places the water lapped at the side of the road.

Sedges, vetches, and grasses grew in profusion, and the air was noisy with the music of coots and cuckoos, whirligig beetles and dragonflies, and the drumming of the snipe. Tufts of solid ground rose above the shallow waters, and swans resting on those little hillocks looked to Will as if they were floating on tiny barges.

There was a scatter of cottages on the edges of the marshes and on small islands here and there. Pointing to a reed-thatched cottage, Will asked Master Tidball why its walls were plastered with smears of what appeared to be cow dung.

"They are drying it for fuel," Tidball said. "There be few trees to chop in this place." He pointed to a man walking on stilts, casting his fishing line into the marsh. "Fens be strange, watery places. And the folk who live here be strange folk." Cocking one eyebrow and lowering his voice so Will had to lean in, he said, "Why, I have heard tales of web-footed people in these fens, of witches and demons who raise hail and tempests and hurtful weather, of ghostly monks chanting in the ruins of their priories."

Will stiffened.

"As we travel, watch for the giant Tom Hickathrift, who prowls these fens," Tidball continued. "Cruel, he is, with the strength of twenty men, and he devours little children." Tidball scratched his nose and spat over the side. "Folk like us would stand no chance against Tom Hickathrift."

Will was silent after that, and watchful.

They stopped at sunset. Will pulled the wagon into a dry spot. He and Master Tidball climbed down and stretched, waiting for Fitz and Benjamin to catch up.

"Master Tidball," said Will, "I ask you again for my wages."

"Fitz is the man to see."

"Nay, Fitz said there is no money for wages."

"I will attend to him. In the meantime, see to the horse."

Will unhitched Solomon and set him loose to find

his supper. Then Will set himself loose, his legs itchy from the hours on the wagon seat. He kicked and jumped and ran west into the sunset, waving his jerkin and shouting, "I be the swiftest runner in the county! None can o'ertake me, and they will choke in the cloud of my dust!"

The flat land offered a fine view of dark lowering clouds, below which the sun fell until it was gone from out of the sky and there was only a rim of gold, and then finally only the memory of gold. The very air was aglow. Will's breath caught in his chest.

Once it began to darken, he ran back to the wagon, where Tidball, Benjamin, and Fitz were gathered. The creature Greymalkin joined them and sat in silence. They built no fire but ate cold pork pie that Fitz brought out from the wagon. Wages were scarce, Will reflected, but leastwise Master Tidball was feeding their bellies again.

"I hear the fiendish Black Dog still roams hereabout," Tidball said through a mouthful of pie. "A giant hound he is, with eyes like blazing fire. In the dark of night you cannot see him but can hear the *pad-pad-pad* of his paws coming ever closer and closer. *Pad-pad-pad,*" he repeated. "Closer and closer. *Pad-pad-pad.*"

The creature leapt up, wrapped her cloak about her, and hurried into the wagon.

Wisps of fog passed over the moon. Will pulled his jerkin on, then lay down and curled around himself for warmth. He thought about the story Benjamin had told him and the questions he still had. The night was black enough, but Will squeezed his eyes shut to make it darker still.

"Sir Juggler," he whispered to Benjamin, "I have been pondering what you told me, and I bethink me I might rather die by the wall than live blind."

"*Facile est dicere,* young Sparrow, it is easy to say. But 'tis difficult to give up the habit of living." Benjamin went on to tell Will how he had learned his juggling, there by the wall of the city. He took to begging for coins and paid small boys to buy leather balls for him at the market fair. He threw the balls low and close to his body to begin and practiced for hours every day. "What else had I to do with my time? At first I was fearful—I trembled and boggled and the balls fell *nolens volens,* willy-nilly, and hit me on the head, dropping useless at my feet, and the boys fetched them back. But I practiced until my arms ached and my fingers grew raw. People stopped to watch, and my cap filled with coins. And so *aud sum,* I am here."

"Aye, but are you not sorry that you cannot see to read and to write? Do you curse God and fortune and the pox?"

"*Me iudice*, in my opinion, life is like juggling," said Benjamin. "Things come at you—balls, clubs, knives, sorrow, loss. Either you stand there and let them hit you or you throw them back *pugnis et calcibus*, with all your might.

"Now *acta est fabula*, the story is over. God grant you pleasing dreams." He pulled his cloak over his face and began to snore.

Will thought about begging and juggling and suffering from the pox. He thought of his own life and the hungry children at the fair. He himself had had much thrown at him, but still he was more fortunate than some. *The fortunate Will Sparrow*, he said to himself. *Certes, an odd notion.*

He wrapped himself more securely in his cloak and lay watching for giant men and dogs as long as he could keep his eyes open but finally fell asleep to the eerie lullaby of the honking of the swans.

Suddenly out of the darkness came unearthly howls and the sound of giant footsteps. *Pad-pad-pad. Pad-pad-pad.*

"Hist, Sparrow, what is that?" Benjamin asked in a husky whisper.

Will jumped up, his heart pounding as the steps drew nearer. *Pad-pad-pad* and ghastly howling. The Black Dog! He stood frozen in fear.

Fitz clambered out from beneath the wagon and stood next to Will, and the girl poked her head out the door, calling, "What? What? What?" All then was quiet until the sound came again. *Pad-pad-pad.* Will shuddered and backed up against the wagon.

Benjamin's head swiveled as if he were smelling the air. "'Tis coming from that direction," he said, pointing.

A bit of moonlight showed not a black dog or demon of any sort but instead Tidball, stomping his good foot and thumping the ground with his walking stick.

"A pox on you, you pitiless villain!" Fitz shouted. "The Devil take your evil jest. You near sent us into apoplexy."

The man only laughed. "You cowards!" he cried. "Afeared of a cripple and his walking stick!" He dropped to the ground and howled once more before saying, "Ah, I be a jolly prankster indeed. You, young Sparrow, you are not a cringing coward. You admire a merry jest."

Will thought it had the smell of a cruel prank rather than a jest, but Tidball's words felt like an arm around Will's shoulders. They were together against the others— the sound versus the odd. He threw a weak smile to the man. "'Twas a merry jest indeed, Master Tidball."

The girl came out from the wagon and, mumbling, lay down next to Fitz. Belike oddities did not understand jests, Will thought. Tidball yawned and closed his eyes, but Will stayed awake long into the night.

THIRTEEN

OF THE CREATURE GREYMALKIN AND
THE GIRL GRACE WYSE

IN THE morning fog everything was but shapes and shadows. Will relieved himself against a willow tree. His stream steamed in the cold—it would be autumn soon, and then winter. His purse was empty. Would he be on the road once more, eating frozen berries and sleeping on the ground? Would he never be safe and warm and dry? Shivering at the thought, he brushed cold droplets from his skin and clothing and dried Solomon's coat with a handful of reeds.

Tidball, under the wagon, awoke and bellowed in pain. Will helped him to slide out. "'Swounds," he said, "but this ankle of mine troubles me no end. Belike 'tis due to last night's merriment. Today I ride inside the wagon. You, boy, take the wild cat."

Muttering, "I am ne'er a cat," the girl jumped out of the wagon and climbed onto the seat. She was wrapped in her blue cloak and had pulled the hood forward, hiding her face.

Will bade farewell to Benjamin, who would walk with Fitz again, and strode to the wagon. He stared at the creature. Never had he been so close to it—to her. She was not so very big or dangerous-looking, huddled there in her cloak. When he climbed onto the seat, she looked away. He picked up the reins, and they traveled an hour or two in silence.

Will was unsure and ill at ease, but it had been a long, lonely ride, and there was much farther to go yet. He sought diversion. Mayhap, he thought, 'twould be possible to talk to her now that he could not see her face for her cloak. He might pretend she was a person and not an oddity at all.

He cleared his throat several times and squeaked, "What means the name *Greymalkin*?"

She said nothing.

"Did your mother give you that name?"

Still she said nothing.

They rode a mile or more before Will said, "Will you not speak to me at all?"

There was more silence, broken only by the lonesome sound of frogs croaking in the fog.

Will grew bored, restless, and eager for company—even hers. Finally he said, " 'Tis right dreary and wearying to be riding here as if alone. And so, both to occupy myself and ensure your attention, I shall sing in a loud voice every rude tavern song I learned at the inn." He sang, "I pray now attend to this ditty, a merry and frolicsome say" and "Come drink to me and I shall drink to you." He bellowed, "Pinch him, pinch him, black and blue," "What hap had I to marry a shrew," and "A soldier's a man, life's but a span, why, then, let a soldier drink!" finishing with a chorus of belches. Still the girl said nothing, and the silence grew as heavy as a sodden coat about Will's shoulders.

As the day grew older, the mist cleared, revealing the road that stretched on and on, held back from the pools and marshes by willow-banked dikes. In the distance a hill rose from the flat land, topped by towers taller than Will had ever seen or imagined.

"Think you, Greymalkin," asked Will, "that those towers reach nigh unto heaven?"

She made no answer.

The nearer they rode to Ely, the taller the towers grew. The wagon climbed the hill to arrive in the town itself. Will stood at the base of the towers, looking up, and he could not see the tops. 'Twas Ely Cathedral. "Fie upon it," Will muttered. "God himself must have added the topmost stones, for no mortal man could climb so high."

"Aye," the girl said, and Will was pleased that he had finally moved her to say something, even if it were only *aye*.

The town was full of the fair, with booths and stalls all around the walls, at the gateway, in the streets, and on the wharves on the river. The place was bustling with merchants setting up. Stilt walkers and tumblers and dancers with bells on their shoes cavorted past to the sounds of tents flapping, merchants calling, lute players and flute players and little boys with tin whistles. Some folks had to make do with cloth laid on the ground to display their wares, but Will found a space next to the ale stall at the edge of the market square where they could erect their booth and park their wagon behind instead of leaving it in the field outside the fair.

Soon Fitz and Benjamin arrived. Benjamin bade them farewell, saying he would ply his trade at the east end of the fair but would return ere the fair was over if he chose to travel with them further. Fitz and Will carried boxes and barrels from the wagon to the booth. Tidball sat on a box and directed them with his walking stick until he fell asleep, whereupon Fitz, looking up at the late-day sky, said, "I must away. Finish unpacking, and I will return as soon as I . . . anon. I will return anon." He scuttled away.

A soft voice came from inside the wagon. "Hist, who be out there?"

"Ah, Greymalkin, I knew you could speak when you wished to," Will said.

She looked out. "Oh, 'tis you, rude boy," she said as she jumped down. "Know this: I shall not speak to you so long as you call me Greymalkin. 'Tis a name for a cat."

"What then?"

"You may call me Grace Wyse, for such I have now named myself. I have long been thinking of a fitting name. I had considered calling myself Wynefred or Millicent or Thomasine, but cats might be called such, might they not? I have met nary a cat with a name like Grace Wyse." She sighed. In contentment? Will wondered. In sorrow? In resignation? How could he know the thoughts of such a creature? She peered at him. "Grace Wyse," she said. "Do you not think it a fine name for a person?"

There was that face, ginger haired, with pointed chin and green eyes, right before him. And he could not help but ask, "Why is your face as it is? Was your mam frightened by a cat? Or is it mayhap a witch's curse?"

The girl's shoulders slumped. "I find I do not wish to speak to you after all, rude boy." She hopped back into the wagon and closed the door.

To Will's mind she was a creature—a fairly tame and harmless creature, but a creature nonetheless. However, she spoke like a person and acted like a person and thought herself a person, and he had reminded her that she was, well, different. Very different. An oddity. He was surprised to find he was sorry for what he had said, but he was reluctant to say so.

Lying came easily to Will, and thieving. To humble himself and apologize was more difficult, but he would not leave it this way. He cleared his throat loudly and with a croak began to sing "Greensleeves," a song he knew well, but with his own words:

> Alas, Grace Wyse, you do me wrong
> To cast me off discourteously,
> For I have labored oh so long
> Delighting in your company.
>
> Grace Wyse is all my joy,
> Grace Wyse is my delight,
> Grace Wyse is my heart of gold,
> Who but my lady Grace Wyse.

Will had sung loudly enough to be heard within the wagon, but Grace did not return. Well, no matter, he thought, he did not truly want to speak with her anyway, oddity that she was. He finished the unpacking and setting up and then sat to watch Tidball sleep, imitating his snorts, puffs, and whistles to pass the time.

Evening had come before Fitz returned. His clothes were disarranged, his hair dusty and tousled, and his right eye bruised and beginning to darken. He let out a soft moan as he dropped to the ground and wiped blood from his lip with the hem of his shirt.

Tidball snorted himself awake. "Have you been brawling again, Lancelot, you little fool? Can you not control your temper?" To Will he said, "He is a most violent and disagreeable little person, is he not? Beware his moods and fits of ill feeling."

"My wages?" Will whispered to Master Tidball. "You said you would attend to it."

"Fitzgeoffrey, this lad would have his pennies," said Master Tidball. "And supper, I imagine. See to it."

Fitz scowled, but he took a purse from his belt and tossed it to Will. "Go, infant. Bring us supper."

Coins. Many coins. Should he buy supper for them all or take the coins as his wages and run? How far would this many coins take him? At the thought of leaving, he felt a strange clenching in his belly. Mayhap it was but hunger, he thought. Only hunger. Certes he could not run on an empty belly. So it would be supper, and off he set to find foodstuffs both tasty and warm.

This fair was considerably larger than the last. He sauntered slowly through the grassy fields, past silver-smiths, pewter crafters, makers of boots and saddles and swords, sellers of cloth and candles and ale. Here was a field of horses, there stalls of hemp and hops and fragrant herbs. He followed the aromas of roasting pork, currant buns, cinnamon and cloves, deliberating what to buy for supper.

A familiar scent from a perfumer's booth lured him in. Lavender water it was, and it smelled, he realized, like his mother. He closed his eyes and recalled her sweet fragrance and her soft lap. Was it true, as his father said, that she left because of Will? He had been hardly more than a babe. He rubbed his nose to get rid of the smell of her and shook his head to blow the memories away.

Will spent every coin in the purse and returned with pears and cheese, juicy beef ribs, a jug of ale, and the promise of an apple tart when it had done baking. He heard the sounds of laughter and quarrels and music as the other merchants and performers gathered by their fires, sharing food and company. The oddities as usual kept to themselves, knowing themselves not welcome at anyone's fire. Will found it easier to stay and eat with them than to seek other company, especially given the beef ribs. Master Tidball waved the food away, but the rest ate in tired silence.

"I have someut to say," the girl said in a small voice, after the apple tart arrived and had been eaten. She cleared her throat and continued a bit louder. "I did not mind so much being Greymalkin the cat when I was young. It seemed a game to act the cat. But now I be Grace Wyse, person, not cat, and wish to be called such. Grace Wyse, an it please you."

Tidball grunted and said, "Call yourself Greymalkin or Grace or Godiva—we know what you are, would you just accept it."

"I do not know what I be—mayhap only God knows—but I know what I am not: I am in no part cat. I will tell no more lies and never again act the cat. Or the beast." She stood proudly and climbed into the wagon.

Tidball grunted again and then rose. "I be meeting an important personage in town. Lancelot Fitzgeoffrey, hie you into the booth to guard my treasures. And you, boy, stay here with the wagon." He hobbled away.

Fitz stood and scratched his head sleepily. "The important personage likely is an innkeeper with brandy-wine and a soft bed. You will not often find our Master Tidball sleeping on the cold ground."

Will could not stay silent at such slander. "Why must you ever find fault with the man? He employs us and feeds us, and we owe him gratitude, not—"

"You, boy," said Fitz with a lift of an eyebrow, "have no more brains than a wood louse." He spat, stretched again, and left.

FOURTEEN

CONCERNING SAMUEL'S DISTRESS,

WILL'S NEW CHARGE, AND

THOUGHTS ABOUT HAM

PLAGUE! THE plague is here!" Will heard the cries from behind the spice merchant's stall the next morning. They were picked up by the stall holders and then the visitors. "Plague!"

People began to push and shove away. Will pushed against them, toward the sounds. He feared the sores and buboes, cramping belly, and death that the plague was said to bring, but he was right curious.

"Nay! Nay!" called a man coming from the scene. "'Tis but a fever. Not the plague." He grabbed people by their sleeves to stop their running off in panic and shouted louder. "The apothecary has come! He says 'tis but a fever!"

Will crept around behind the stall where the uproar

had begun, and there was Samuel Knobby's cart! The Duchess, squealing like, well, a pig, was tied to one of the wheels. Will stuck his head over the side of the cart and looked down. Samuel, his face red and shiny with sweat, thrashed about. Samuel!

"A putrid fever, I say," said a man in black leaning over the cart. "He must be bled regularly and dosed with mustard, garlic, and St. John's wort. And he should be kept warm and still for nigh onto a seven-night if he is to recover. Is there somewhere within doors where he might shelter?"

No one answered. Finally the apothecary sighed and said, "I have an attic where he might stay, but someone must pay my fee and a bit extra for his board."

There was much discussion and consternation, but finally someone passed a cap around and coins were thrown in with many a clink and a clank. Why did these folk care enough to turn over their pennies? Will wondered. Mayhap it was but a trick, and Samuel would take the money and run off. That was belike what the villainous tooth puller would do. But to the boy's surprise, the money was given to the apothecary, who counted it and nodded.

Samuel Knobby began wriggling. He mumbled words no one could understand. When his eyes alighted on Will, he grabbed the boy's arm and pointed to the ground.

"I believe," said Will, "that he is asking about the Duchess. Can she go with him?"

"Where might this Duchess be?" the apothecary asked, smoothing his hair and straightening his robe.

"The Duchess is his pig," Will answered, "the smartest pig in the world, he says, and clean, and—"

"A pig!" the apothecary growled. "No pig. I will have trouble enough explaining the man himself to my wife."

Samuel thrashed harder.

"But the Duchess goes everywhere with Samuel. How will she fare without him? Who will feed her? And play with her? Splash her with water and practice her tricks and . . ."

Everyone looked at Will, and he knew why. They expected him to do it. But he cared for no one but himself and nothing but his belly.

Samuel grabbed Will's hand. The boy looked about for someone, anyone, who would take the pig, but all eyes—blue eyes and green eyes and brown, candid eyes and hooded eyes, sad eyes and laughing eyes, young eyes and old—were on him. Fie upon it, Will Sparrow would have to do it, take on the care and feeding of the Duchess while Samuel Knobby recovered. From Samuel he had learned something of caring for a pig. He supposed he could do it. He had, after all, been taking fine care of Solomon these many days. The boy sighed a mighty sigh. Although he liked it not, he would have to do it. And the Duchess nuzzled his ankle, as if she knew. Samuel and the cart were trundled to the apothecary shop, and Will led the Duchess away.

As they neared the wagon, Will heard Master Tidball shouting, "You will, you impudent wench! Stubborn as a goat you are, but you will! Folk pay to see the wild girl, half cat, and see her they will, or you will stay in here until your bones turn to dust!" He slammed and barred the wagon door as the Duchess snorted over to sniff at his clothing—looking for treats, Will knew.

Master Tidball barked, "What does that swine here!"

Will explained, and Tidball said, "Keep the dirty thing away from me," and he kicked at her with his good foot while standing on his bad foot, which caused him to twist the ankle anew. "A pox on you all!" he cried. "I am plagued like Job!" He turned to the wagon, unbarred the door, pulled the girl out, and climbed in himself, remaining out of the way the rest of the day.

Between the creature's—Grace's, he amended—stubbornness and Fitz's brawling and ill humor, it was no wonder the man's temper flared at times, Will thought. *I am the only one who does not torment him.*

Will and the Duchess sat in the sunshine and shared

an apple Will had nicked from a fruitmonger's stall. Grace, watching, said, "I hate pigs."

"Know you many pigs?" Will asked.

Grace did not answer but said only, "I hate everyone."

"Nay, you do not."

"I do."

"Do you hate Benjamin?"

"Nay, I be most fond of Benjamin. He says that being blind, he can see me more clearly than others do. And I do not hate you. Does that please you?"

Will felt a sudden warmth but said, "Nay, I care not what you think of me."

"You are a stupid boy."

The Duchess rolled over and snorted with happiness. *Indeed I am, sometimes,* Will thought, *for now I am charged with the tending of a pig.* He frowned and spat apple seeds into the dirt.

For days following, Fitz trumpeted the marvels in the wonder room and collected pennies from the curious. Inside the booth, Grace Wyse sat on the chair on the platform, her arms crossed.

Will walked the fair, calling folk to the booth as he had heard Fitz call. He tended Solomon the horse, dusted the oddities, polished the wagon, and watched the comings and goings in the booth. He was surprised by the number of folks who would pay to see a dead sea monster and an odd chicken. People in fine doublets and ruffs, padded silks and satin capes, russet homespun and frayed linen, lined up for entry. The usual swarms of children in rags crowded about, thrusting out their empty hands, crying, "Good sir, a crust of bread, an it please you" and "Gentles, my mam be sick and the little ones burnin' with fever. I beg help." No one heeded them. A man in velvet doublet and polished sword kicked a small girl out of his way, which made her cry and his raspberry-silked companion giggle.

'Twas his good fortune, Will thought once again, to be fed and employed, even if it were but as hireling of the monstermonger and there looked to be no more wages coming his way. He realized he had stopped asking about wages. His belly was full and his days occupied, but what about when the weather turned foul? Were there still fairs in the winter? If not, what then would he do? What would happen to him? But as long as the sun shone, he was able to push the worries away.

When he could absent himself from Master Tidball and his duties, Will attended to the Duchess. He found a bit of scrubby woodland amidst the marshes and the mires outside the town, where he took her to hunt for acorns and pignuts, mushrooms and worms. Dragging his feet and muttering, he told her over and over that he did not choose to be caring for her but it was necessary until Samuel came back. She listened with her ears erect and her tail spinning in circles, and she would not be dismissed or ignored. Instead she often sat at his side and looked at him so intelligently, Will swore the pig was waiting for him to say something of importance, something she would understand and remember.

One day as the pig and the boy lay in companionable silence, Will, knowing she would not argue or scold, opened his heart to her. "Fie, Duchess, I be liar and thief, unloved and unlovable, and I have no Samuel to look out for me as you do, so I must care for myself and you as well."

He felt a bit silly at first, talking so to a pig, but soon grew more easy. He told her of where he had been, how he came to be here with her, and how strange he felt traveling with oddities. "I do not belong with them, yet I had no choice but to join them for a time. Master Tobias left me for London, for Bartlemas Fair. 'Tis a wonder, Bartlemas Fair, so Master Tidball says."

And the Duchess, having been there once with Samuel, grunted in agreement.

With light heart Will watched her roll in the green

herbs and splash in the water he poured to cool her. "We must have a song," he said, and so they did, one he had learned at the inn.

> Tomorrow the Fox will come to town,
> Keep, keep, keep, keep, keep:
> Tomorrow the Fox will come to town,
> O keep you all well there.

> I must desire you neighbors all
> To halloo the fox out of the hall,
> And cry as loud as you can call,
> O keep you all well there.

"Nay, Duchess," Will said, "we should have a pig song. I will make a pig song." He stood and danced around her, singing:

> Tomorrow the pig will come to town,
> Whee, whee, whee, whee, whee,
> Tomorrow the pig will come to town
> And visit the Ely fair.

> Fairgoers come, come one, come all,
> To watch the pig play with cards and ball
> And call as loud as you can call,

Whee, whee, whee, whee, whee,
When you visit the Ely fair.

The song pleased him so much that he shouted the next verse to the winds:

Her snout is long, her eye is round,
She's the biggest porker pound for pound,
And she makes the most unlovely sound,
Whee, whee, whee, whee, whee,
Here at the Ely fair.

Will swore that the Duchess smiled in pleasure.

The singing and the making of the song tired him, and he lay down with his head on the pig's surprisingly firm, warm, bristly side, which smelled of dust and powder and woolly thyme. He could hear her heart beat. Strange, he thought; he had no mother, no father, no friend, but for the moment he had the Duchess. It was enough.

The next morn dawned rainy and cool. Few people ventured through the damp to the fair, and even fewer found the oddities booth. "I have business elsewhere," Tidball said, leaning heavily on his walking stick. "Do not think you can grow lax whilst I be gone. I be counting the pennies when I return."

As soon as Tidball turned a corner, Fitz said to Will, "I must be off. See to the girl. Do not leave her alone." And he, too, left.

Will grumbled. He was not only pig keeper but also keeper of the wild girl. Or Grace Wyse, as she now insisted. Must he do everything? He would not stay and be the only one to work. He huffed in irritation as he fetched Grace from the wagon. "Come with me."

"Where?"

"Somewhere else, somewhere not here. Come."

Grace followed Will and the Duchess to a quiet spot away from the fair. They found shelter beneath a tree, breathing deeply of the damp, green, mossy smell of the woods. The Duchess poked and prodded the strange creature in the blue cloak, but once she determined there were no apples about the person, she curled up next to the blue cloak, snorted once, and fell asleep.

Grace, frowning, looked down at the pig but did not move away.

"Samuel thinks pigs are smarter and more well-mannered than people," Will told her.

"Mayhap he is right," Grace said. "A pig has ne'er laughed at me or called me names." She reached out carefully and, with one finger, touched the Duchess on her snout. "I thought 'twould be bristly, but 'tis soft," she said, "like fine cloth." She watched the pig sleep for a moment and then said, "I believe I do not hate this pig. She does not think me odd or ugly or indeed any different from you."

"What, Grace, what . . . I mean, what . . ." Will stumbled around the words. "What is it like having . . . being, you know, a cat-faced girl, a—"

"Creature? Oddity? Monster?" Will could see Grace frown, and he feared he had once again insulted her. But she said, " 'Tis at times pitiable, and ever burdensome." She sighed. "Now and again I pretend my face is a mask and not really me at all, just a mask, and I am behind it, apple-cheeked and ordinary. But 'tis all I know. Can you say what 'tis like being Will Sparrow?"

Will Sparrow, liar and thief, knobby kneed and undersized, unloved and unlovable? 'Twas what he was. To say what it was like? He shrugged. There was no saying.

At last the clouds moved by, the rain stopped, and birds and squirrels began to bustle. "We must haste back to the fair afore Master Tidball returns," Will said, and he, Grace, and the Duchess began the walk back.

"Where be you headed?" Grace asked.

He looked at her quizzically. "Back to the booth, am I not?"

"Nay, I mean after all this. How did you come to be here? And where be you going to?"

"Nowhere. I'm going *from*," he said, as he had said

to Nell Liftpurse before. And he told Grace of his mother leaving, of his father and the inn, of the prospect of being a chimney sweep. He was at ease in the telling—belike talking to the Duchess had loosened his tongue.

"Be they still after you?"

Will considered this. "Nay, likely not."

"Then you are not going *from* anymore. Where be you going *to*? Even a sparrow sometime alights."

Sparrow? He frowned but then bethought himself. Grace likely did not mean to insult him, and it was a good question. He had been on the run and on the road nigh on three weeks now, going where the road went. He did not choose but was like a twig caught in the current and propelled downstream: from his father to the inn to Hieronymous Munster and the conjurer and Tidball. Where *was* he going to?

"Will Sparrow, look!" Grace cried. She held aloft a tiny twig on which perched a beetle with wide stripes of green and gold.

" 'Tis indeed most colorful," Will said. "Mayhap Master Tidball would display—"

"Nay!" Grace shouted, flinging the twig and the beetle away. "No displays. This beetle should live free, not caged like me, like the mermaid baby." She stood looking into the distance as if she could see where the beetle had flown. "I grieve for the mermaid baby, Will

Sparrow. She has grown tousled and worn. Her hair is tattered and her tail coming loose."

"No doubt Master Tidball will see her put right."

"She is a person, fish tail or no, and should not be floating in a bottle from fair to fair. I know what 'tis like to be displayed all unwilling."

"The mermaid baby is not alive."

"Still, she should not spend forever in a bottle on a shelf. I would bury her myself, but the flask is too heavy." She looked at Will, her eyes wide and expectant.

Annoyed by her unspoken request, he ran ahead, spinning and jumping, while Grace and the Duchess trailed along behind. No more was said. *Let the mermaid baby sleep in her flask in the booth,* Will thought. Master Tidball was his employer and his ally. Will would not choose to cross the man as Grace did.

The nights were growing cooler. Grace stayed in the wagon, and Master Tidball took to sleeping each night at a nearby inn. Fitz built a fire before he headed for his place in the booth, and Will and the Duchess curled up next to it. Many a night he had reminded himself that he cared for no one and nothing, but one night, listening to the Duchess snore a small, porcine snore, he decided it was no longer true. *Mayhap,* he thought, *I shall say I care for no one but myself and nothing but my belly, and the Duchess a bit, and maybe even Grace a little.* The notion made him either pleased or irritated, he was not certain which.

On an especially cold night Will huddled close to the pig for warmth. He woke to the appetizing aroma of ham. Or bacon. He sniffed deeply. What fortunate person was eating ham in the middle of the night? Will's mouth watered. He sniffed again. It was the Duchess, lying as close as she could to the fire, her warm body giving off the aroma of, well, ham. Of course, he thought, the Duchess *was* ham. And bacon. Roast pork and pigs' trotters. Chops and sausages. Could he ever eat such foods again? He sighed. Fie upon it, this tending of a thing brought unforeseen consequences. He would be certain never to tend a herring or a goose or an apple tart, else he might find himself with naught to eat.

FIFTEEN

REGARDING GRACE'S TROUBLE AND

WILL'S RELUCTANCE

THE NEXT morning brought more damp and bluster. The fair would be late in starting. Will missed the activity of the road. His legs and his mind were restless. He craved something to do, something adventurous.

Will tied the Duchess to the wheel of the wagon—he could do with some time alone—and started off. But there was Grace, peeping from the wagon door. She had spoken little to him since he had ignored the plight of the mermaid baby. Mayhap he could appease her with an invitation. "Hist, Grace Wyse. Come with me. Let this fair sleep today while we see what the town has to offer."

"And let the town see me?" Grace shook her head *no* and *nay* and *ne'er*. "Not with this face of mine. 'Tis but inviting trouble."

Will watched the large green eyes in her cat's face grow sad. "I have grown somewhat fond of your face, for it be gentle and friendly," he told her. "Mayhap others would feel the same if you gave them the chance." He lifted one eyebrow in query.

"Foolish boy. You see me every day. 'Tis different for those who encounter this face for the first time." Yet she agreed to go with him. She wrapped herself in her blue cloak, pulled the hood down to hide her face, and followed Will through the deserted fair and farther into the town.

Dominating the town was the great central tower of the cathedral, and Will, remembering his wonder when first they had arrived, bade Grace look up and up and up. "Belike angels perch there and watch over us," Grace said.

"Belike," said Will, though he misdoubted it.

They peeked into the windows of a tailor's shop and admired the bolts of cloth and what Grace said were crimping irons for ruffs. Will rubbed grime from the window of a lawyer's chambers and they peered in, but they could see nothing beyond a desk and chair and wooden chests. An apothecary's shop held shelves of glass vessels filled with mysterious things brightly colored or brown, liquid or solid, in large pieces or powdered. The apothecary! Did Samuel lie above? Will looked through the open door but saw no one inside to ask.

Next stood a fine inn, the Lamb, its plaster stained with mud and wet, promising warmth and warm food inside. Grace and Will stood a moment in the fragrant steam. People passing on the street paid scant attention to the small boy and the smaller girl cloaked in blue until a cold wind blew the hood back from her face.

Someone passing shouted, "God have mercy, look at the creature!" and his companions did just that, pointing and laughing or shrieking in fright. One woman called, "Alack, alack, such a pitiful thing!" and Will thought perhaps Grace would mind that most of all.

A gaggle of half-grown boys stumbled toward them. "Let us go, Will, I pray you, back to the wagon," Grace said, pulling on his sleeve, but the boys surrounded them.

"How now, Rowly," hollered a boy with a runny nose, "here is someone yet more ugly than you!"

A boy in patched doublet grabbed Grace's arm and looked into her face. "By God, the lass has need of a barber!"

"Are you this shaggy elsewhere?" another boy asked as he pulled at her cloak while Grace yelped and struggled.

Will stood still. What could he do? The boys were so many and so big, and his nose still hurt from his encounter with Alf back in Stamford.

From the doorway of the Lamb came a roar. Master Tidball, red-faced and raging, strode into the tumult. "Away with you, you scurvy rascals!" he shouted, swinging his stick. "You wretched worms, you slugs, you curs!" The boys took off running and jeering.

Grace clung to Tidball's doublet. He pulled her hood forward, but not before Will saw her tears. *Fie upon it,* he thought, he had forgotten that she was but a young thing. She looked so odd and was so well-spoken that he often considered her some strange otherworldly being. The creature, he thought her. But she was, in sooth, a child—a person, as he was. He kicked at the ground.

Master Tidball frowned at Will, and the boy could see the muscles in the man's jaw tighten. "Froggenhall should have added cowardly to his list of your attributes," Tidball said. He grabbed Grace's arm and pulled her back toward the fair.

Will said nothing, although he thought, *Nay, not cowardly.* He had wanted to help, truly he had, but he hadn't known how. And his nose did pain him. He followed Tidball and Grace with slow and heavy steps.

The weather was clearing, and crowds were returning to the fair, but the oddities booth was deserted and Fitz nowhere to be seen. "Lancelot Fitzgeoffrey!" Master Tidball bellowed. "Fitz, you minnow, you insect, where be you?" He thumped the ground with his stick. "The Devil take him, belike he is brawling again. Why do I abide him?"

Tidball shoved Grace into the booth. "Go bedeck yourself in some wild garb and make ready to frighten folk. And you, Sparrow, apply yourself to something useful. Convince folk to come and pay their pennies."

Will strode away, calling, "Come and see. Oddities and prodigies of all sorts here are seen. A one-eyed pig and a three-legged chicken. Behold true wonders and marvels for only a penny."

"Sparrow!" Another bellow from Master Tidball brought Will back to the booth. "Nay. 'Tis Greymalkin who will draw them in. Listen and then do as I do." He swept his cap from his head, bowed, and called, "Gentlemen and gentlewomen, goodmen and gossips, come and see! Mark me, here be a monstrous child!" He paced back and forth before the booth, catching folks by their sleeves. "She be half wild cat and half human, a creature never before seen on England's shores. Be she of a strange and unknown race? Or is her monstrous condition a curse or punishment for sins? We know not. She be a wonder and a mystery, in sooth. Come and behold."

A knot of well-dressed gentlefolk gathered and paid Tidball their coins. "That is how 'tis done," he said to Will as the gentles entered the booth, shoving past the begging children crowded there. "Now go you and do likewise."

Before Will walked on, the fine folk had emerged. One man in a yellow taffety doublet and mouse-colored hose, his ruff all aquiver with his irritation, grabbed Tidball's arm. "You, sirrah, are a liar and a cheat, taking money falsely from honest gentlefolk. No monster waits inside but a girl sitting quietly, giving us her back. She does not roar nor rumble nor even show her face. A poor monster indeed." Tidball returned his coins, and his party left, muttering.

Tidball, his face as red as an October apple, hurried into the booth. "You pathetical axwaddle!" he shouted. "Get you up and do something fierce!" Will heard a slap, and a cry from Grace.

Will was shocked by Tidball's sudden cruelty and surprised that Grace would continue in her defiance, no matter the cost. He himself would be more careful not to annoy Master Tidball. But as he proceeded through the fair, calling folk to come see the oddities and wonders, Will did not mention Grace. Let folk be satisfied with the three-legged chicken, he decided.

At long last the day was over and Will found his way back to the booth. Fitz, sporting a great black eye, sat with his back against the wagon wheel. "No supper today, no Tidball, no Grace," he said, and he closed his eyes.

Will's belly rumbled. "Where are they?"

"He has taken her into the town again," said Fitz.

"To sup with rich gentlemen?"

Fitz shrugged. "He takes her wherever he will. She belongs to him." He stood, spat, and limped off.

What did that mean? Was Tidball her father? Silence reigned, and the next thing Will knew, it was morning and Solomon the horse was nibbling grass near his ear.

Grace, he saw, was standing, leaning against the wagon, clutching a loaf of bread. "You, Grace Wyse, fare you well?" he asked.

"Aye, indeed, how else should I fare?" She tore off a hunk of her bread, handed a piece to the Duchess and one to Will, and sat down next to him. "Master Tidball," she said, "has gone into the booth with Fitz. He said you are a lazy cur and not worth your wages."

"Which are naught," Will said. Autumn was here, the nights growing longer and the days chillier. The cold crawled below his shirt and bit the tip of his nose. Where would he be come winter? Would Master Tidball continue to care for the oddities then? And he remembered Fitz's statement of the night before. "Is Master Tidball your father?" Will asked Grace.

"Him?" She spat on the ground. "Ne'er! I would rather this pig were my father. He says my mam sold me to him when I was but five summers old."

Sold, as he had been. "Then why do you not leave him?"

"Master Tidball says I am free to go when I have repaid what he gave my mam, else he will call the sheriff and I be sent to prison. But I have no money and no way to earn such, for he gives me only food and a place to sleep. I look never to get away."

So Grace had no wages either. It appeared that Fitz kept all their earnings. "Could not you steal away and—"

"Foolish boy! Think you I could travel unnoticed? A cat-faced girl?" Tears filled her green eyes, and she wiped them with the hem of her dress.

Will watched her, an unlovely child sold like a sausage. He was silent for a moment, thinking of his lost mother and the father who had sold him for ale. Were ever two babes more unfortunate? "Do you remember your mam at all?" he asked finally.

"Nay. What I remember is waking on the floor of

the wagon, cringing in the corner, with frightful beasts staring at me from bottle and shelf." She shivered. "I was afeared of them at first, monstrous creatures born and unborn, dead and undead. But now I think they watch over me, the one-eyed pig and the mermaid baby and the others. They do not care that I am ugly. They care for me and keep me from being lonely, they and Fitz." Grace smiled. "And you, now that you be here."

Will looked at her for a moment. A cat. A sad and friendly cat. "I do not think you ugly," said Will, surprised but knowing it to be true. "Just somewhat more bewhiskered than most." He rubbed his chin. He longed to be bewhiskered himself, but his chin was still smooth and hairless.

Grace snuffled, and then she began to cry in earnest. "The poor wee mermaid baby . . . she is more forlorn even than I. She should be laid to rest, Will Sparrow. I would bury her, and I would have you help me." She laid her hand on his arm. "I pray you. Together we could carry her flask, though it be heavy indeed."

"Nay, she do be Master Tidball's," Will said, his voice squeaking. "I would not discontent him."

She started to speak again, but Will, pushing her hand away, said, "Nay, Grace, I will not." The morning had grown brighter, and more people were about. Grace slipped silently into the booth.

Will scratched the sleeping Duchess on her bristly back and tied her to the wagon. "I must go to Master Tidball and see what he would have me do. You stay here, Duchess, and guard—" What was there worth guarding? "The wheels, Duchess. Guard the wheels, for we will ne'er move again without them." He patted her on her snout, enjoying its warmth and softness, and took a few steps. He stopped and turned back again. "And the girl, Duchess, pray look after the girl."

SIXTEEN

ABOUT A RELUCTANT RETURN TO

THIEVERY AND A SURPRISING DISCOVERY

NOT MANY steps later Will stopped as a cart rumbled up in front of him. The carter jumped out and made his way to the ale stall. "A felon," Will heard the carter say to the alewife, "caught thieving here at the fair. I be taking her to the magistrate for punishment." The carter drained his mug and pushed it forward to be filled again.

"You, boy," someone called from the cart. It was a woman with a plump red face, white teeth, sky-blue kirtle under a bodice of buttercup yellow, and fine reddish hair peeping out from beneath a green hat. Nell Liftpurse! "Remember me? We was friends for a bit. You be Master . . . some kind of bird, is that not right?" She beckoned him over.

"Sparrow. I be Will Sparrow." He went closer. Nell's hands were bound tightly to the side of the cart with stout rope.

She spoke quietly. "Aye, Sparrow. Now, Sparrow, I would flee from here, and I pray your assistance. I were kind to you, were I not?"

"You pinched my apples and my blanket," Will said.

"I did? Well, I be right sorry for that, but we compeers of the road, we must help each other, must we not? I pray you, Sparrow, help me. They mean to cut off my ears or my hand or stretch my neck!" Nell's voice shook with fear. "Sparrow, help me!"

The boy sighed. He opened his mouth to say nay, he cared for no one but himself, but then he looked her fully in the face. She reminded him of someone. Something about the eyes and the blue kirtle. He shook the memory away and sighed again. He supposed he would help her, but not too much.

"I will find a knife or shears or some such so you can free yourself. Wait here." He snorted at his words. *Wait here?* Had she a choice?

Will thought he might find a knife or a pair of strong shears ripe for nipping, but he did not fancy sharing Nell Liftpurse's cart or her punishment. Master Tidball and Benjamin had knives, but he did not know where either man could be found, and Fitz carried no knife.

Master Tidball said it was too dangerous for an ill-tempered brawler to have such a thing. Will could not buy—he did not have even a ha'penny and had given up hope of seeing any. Would some shopkeeper allow a puny, dirty, barefoot boy to borrow as valuable a thing as a knife or shears or a small hand ax? Aye, he would like the feel of a hand ax. He could but try.

He searched the stalls. He found drums and battledores, shuttlecocks and pipes, trumpets and comfits and bright-painted dolls, stalls of fine fabrics and rough shoes and hats of painted leather. Ahh, there was a seller of ladies' trifles. A counter ran around three sides of the booth, displaying needles and thread, spoons and shears and amber bracelets. Shears. They would do.

"These are fine shears," Will said to the booth keeper. "Strong enough to sever heavy rope, I vow."

"Indeed," said the man, directing a wary glance at Will's ragged breeches and bare feet. "I ask but a groat for them—a great bargain. See how sharp and finely balanced."

"Good master," Will said, "might I borrow these fine shears for a moment and—"

"Get away," snarled the booth keeper, hands on his hips.

"I will use them gently and return—"

"Away, before I use them to separate your nose from your thieving body!"

Thieving? There it was. He had no choice. He would nip them. The thought of being caught filled him with fright. He had not been thieving these many days. Had he lost the knack?

He had not, and in a wink the shears were tucked into the waistband of his breeches.

Will hurried back to Nell, panting from the effort and the noonday sun. But the cart was gone and Nell with it. He had taken too long. Poor Nell, left to her fate and justice and the mercy of God.

He sat down right there by the road and mopped his sweating face with the tail of his shirt. The shears at his waist pricked him. And he decided to do something he had never before done and never thought to do. He would put the purloined shears back. *Why?* he wondered. He was a liar and a thief, was he not? But his belly was full enough not to depend on what he could steal.

And there were other reasons. He was surprised to find that he didn't want Master Tidball or Benjamin, Grace or the Duchess or even Fitz, to know him for a thief. He didn't want to end like Nell, tied to a cart like a cow for the butcher. And the shopkeeper would certainly suspect him if he discovered the shears missing.

Indeed, returning the shears seemed like exactly the right thing to do.

He meandered through the fair, trying to look upright and innocent, until he was in sight of the booth where he had found the shears. He could not slip them back onto the counter where they had been, for there were too many people about. Instead he merely dropped them into the dirt and kicked them close to the booth before he began once more to move through the fair, calling, "Wonders and marvels, oddities and prodigies, in the booth hard by the ale stall at the west side of the fair," as if that was what he had been about all along.

"That be him!" came a cry behind him. "That be the thief who took my shears!" And the booth keeper grabbed Will's sleeve. "Take him," the man said to an official-looking person in a black hat and a coat of red worsted.

"Shears? Nay, I have no shears," Will said, and it was the truth.

"Bailiff, search him!" the booth keeper cried, spraying spittle about like mist in the wind.

"Search me, an it please you," said Will. "I have no pocket nor pouch, and my purse is as empty as my belly. Where might I hide a pair of shears?"

The red-coated man patted Will's sleeves and looked in his purse. He shook his head. "Nothing. Not even moths."

"I accuse him!" the booth keeper cried. "He must be taken."

"I will go most willingly," Will said, "if you be sure the shears are in sooth missing."

"I have searched carefully," said the booth keeper to the bailiff. "The shears were there, the boy was there, and now the shears are gone."

"You will search again," said the bailiff, pulling Will back to the booth.

The bailiff and the booth keeper searched through the booth and examined all the counters while Will stood somewhat apart, watching.

"They be gone indeed," said the booth keeper, just as a woman standing by said, "What is that glimmer in the dust there?" The glimmer proved to be the shears, lying on the ground under the counter.

"You must have dropped them," said the bailiff, handing them to the booth keeper.

"Ne'er! That ne'er happened!" the booth keeper shouted. "He thieved them and then replaced them."

Everyone looked at Will, who said, "Say you I am a thief and I nip things and then I put them back again? I must be as stupid as a sack of rocks."

The bailiff and the onlookers agreed. The bailiff scolded the booth keeper for wasting his time and left, walking east.

Will prudently headed to the west. "Stay away from my booth!" the booth keeper shouted after him.

Will nodded, relieved to be at liberty and not in the cart with Nell, and determined never to cross paths with the angry man again. "Wonders and marvels," he called as he hurried away, "oddities and prodigies, fine gentlemen. Come and see. In the booth hard by the ale stall."

A fair-haired man in a chestnut doublet was leaning against a cart, watching the rope walker. Will stared. Red boots. The man had red leather boots! Will's toes tingled. He wanted those boots with all his wanting. Why, he could do and be whatever he wished in boots such as those.

A memory tugged at him. At the inn he had run from, a frequent customer had such boots. And fair hair. And a chestnut—He turned to run as the man shouted, "You there, boy, stop! I know you!"

Will ran behind the saddle maker, through a crowd at the spice stall, and behind a purveyor of chickens, hanging by their feet and squawking. He jumped a basket of pears and apples, slid between two women in farthingales near the size of wagons, and knocked over a barrel of brooms and rakes. Past the ale stall he ran, back to the oddities booth, where he dove beneath the wagon.

He looked out and saw red-booted feet move from

the booth to the wagon. He held his breath. Had he been seen?

Fitz's small worn shoes joined the red boots. "Have you seen a boy run through here?" a voice asked, the very same voice that had bid him stop.

"'Twas no boy. 'Twas me," said Fitz.

"Nay, a boy. I chased him though the fair, but I do not know where he has gone."

"'Twas me, I said. Behold, I am still breathless from running." Fitz panted a time or two, said *whew* and *heu,* and panted again. "I be sorry to put you to such trouble," he added, "but knew not what you wanted and ran in fear." Will heard the jingle of coins. "Take this for your pains, good sir, and forgive me."

There was such stillness that Will feared they could hear his pounding heart. Then: "Mayhap I was mistaken," said Red Boots. "I took you for a boy my innkeeper once owned, a runaway, a liar, and a thief. Thought to trade him to the innkeeper for a meal or two. But belike I was mistaken. And in sooth 'tis no matter to me anyway."

"Indeed, sir, I am no boy and have not the breath to do much running, as you easily see."

There was laughter then, and Red Boots said, "Gramercy for the coin. A mug of ale will make me forget I ever saw him . . . er, you." And the red boots strode off.

"You can come out now, stripling," said Fitz after a moment. "He has gone."

Will waited, fearful that Fitz was fooling him and the man was lurking out there to grab him, but he could not stay under that wagon forever. He came slowly out.

Fitz continued. "I would stay close by for a time to make certain the fellow has forgotten you. I will tell Tidball you have a griping of the gut."

"Why are you helping me?"

Fitz raised both his great yellow eyebrows. "I have heard the girl at times laughing at your foolishness. The sound gladdens me."

Will was overcome with surprise at hearing such an unlikely thing from the disagreeable Fitz. And even greater was Will's surprise that he had run to the oddities for safety and protection instead of away. Greatest of all was his surprise at finding refuge there. *The world is full of wonders,* he decided.

SEVENTEEN

WILL STAYED very near the wagon with the Duchess for a day before he felt safe enough to return to the fair.

"Sparrow," Master Tidball greeted him, "I trust your gut will now allow you to work off some of the generous wages I pay you."

Will made to ask, *What wages?* but Tidball stopped him. "No, no. No apologies. Hie you now to the south end of the fair and tell the metalsmith I will see him this night. And hasten right back. You will need to help Fitz, for I have business elsewhere."

Will returned to the wagon to take the Duchess for a brief walk before he joined Fitz at the booth. As he was loosing her from the wheel, there came a familiar voice at his back. "How be you, young Sparrow?"

"Samuel!" Will spun to face him. "Well met, Samuel, well met!" The boy's smile faded at the sight of the pig trainer. Samuel was no longer round nor lardy—indeed, his skin seemed far too big for him. The Duchess saw nothing amiss, it seemed, for she waddled and snorted up to greet him, rubbing her side against his legs. Will thought she would purr if she could.

"Ah, my Porcine Duchess," Samuel crooned, "you have missed me. And I you." He rubbed the pig's head.

"How fare you?" Will asked him.

"The apothecary," Samuel said, "has the notion that I am in need of more rest and less ale. And so the Duchess and I go to my sister and her husband in St. Albans. Lettice's face may be sharp as an ax, and her voice as well, but her heart is soft as her jelly. She will take us in and feed us."

The Duchess prodded the purse on Samuel's belt with her snout. "Looking for apples, be you? Have I yet failed you?" He pulled a slice from the purse, and the Duchess snapped at it greedily. "We will miss the performing life, the Duchess and I," Samuel said to Will. "Mayhap we will do tricks with cards out behind the barn." His eyes grew dim with sadness, as if a candle had suddenly blown out.

Will wished to say something to ease Samuel's pain but could think of no words that would serve. He merely stretched out his empty hands as if offering what he had, which was nothing.

"And we shall miss you, Will Sparrow," Samuel continued. "God keep you safe." From his purse he took a handful of coins. "I have coins still from what the fair folk collected for me. More than the Duchess here and I will need." He poured a few, sticky with apple, into Will's hand. "Find a purveyor of old clothes and get yourself some boots, boy. It be too cold to tread the world with your feet bare."

Will's fists closed on the coins as he stood in silent sadness and regret and astonishment. Samuel stepped away, and the Duchess made to follow him. Then she turned back and rubbed once more against Will's leg, her tail spinning.

Will's heart clenched with a pain he had never known, or perhaps had long forgotten. Longing, loss, sorrow, but something more. Something not sad but happy and warm. Liar and thief though he was, the Duchess trusted him. And more. She loved him. His mam and father could not or would not, but this pig loved him. He threw his arms around her neck and smelled her dusty, herby smell one last time.

In a moment Samuel and the Duchess were walking

away. "God save you, Samuel. And may he look after the world's smartest pig," Will called to them. Samuel raised his cap in farewell and commenced his tuneless caterwauling:

> He turned his face unto the wall
> And death was in him swellin',
> Good-bye, good-bye, to my friends all.
> Be good to Barbra Allen.
>
> When he lay dead and in his grave,
> She heard the death bells knellin';
> And every stroke to her did say:
> Hardhearted Barbra Allen.

Will watched them go. "Phah!" he cried, and he threw a clod of dirt against an empty cart, and then another. "Phah! I will not again do as I am bid! I will do my own bidding!" He would spend Samuel's coins to buy himself a pair of shoes against the winter cold.

The boots at the leatherworkers' stalls were heavy and stiff, and those at the bootmaker's fine and worth more pennies than he had. He stowed Samuel's coins in the purse at his waist and moved on.

In ill humor he watched the archers and the stilt walkers and the acrobats. Nothing diverted him. Finally he returned to the woodland where he and the Duchess had played, and there he lay, face to the sky, muttering all the rude words he knew.

He squinted. One dark cloud passing overhead looked like—yes, like the Duchess. A flying pig in the sky over Ely. He sang to the sky, his changing voice rasping and squeaking:

> Her snout is long, her eye is round,
> She's the biggest porker pound for pound,
> And she makes the most unlovely sound,
> Whee, whee, whee, whee, whee,
> Here at the Ely fair.

And he shed a tear or two.

By then afternoon was nigh. Fitz would be wondering where Will had gone. He stood, smoothed his shirt, and straightened his breeches. He walked back toward the booth, searching for a good excuse for his absence.

"We have a challenger, goodmen!" a voice nearby called. "We have a challenger!"

Indeed? For what? Will went closer. Beneath a tree a crowd whooped and cheered. Will pushed his way through. A giant of a man in rough brown doublet and trunk hose stood with onlookers circled around him.

It appeared there was to be a wrestling match. Who was brave enough to stand up to such a colossus?

A tall man with his paunch stuffed into a ginger doublet cried, "Here he is, the challenger. Can he topple our champion? Come and place your wagers, goodmen. Place your wagers."

The onlookers howled with laughter, and Will struggled to see why. God-a-mercy! The challenger was Fitz. Fitz, with his thick arms and short legs, brawling just as Master Tidball said! Fitz, who stood only as high as the champion's belt! Fitz threw his cap to the ground and removed his doublet, making ready to face the giant.

"The two wrestlers shall meet here in the empty space," the man in ginger announced, "and if one cause the other to let his back or shoulder touch the ground, he is said to have given a fall. If the challenger can avoid a fall for fifteen minutes of the hour, he is called the winner and will receive sixpence as well as a share of the wagers. Should he fell the champion, he shall receive a shilling and a full half of the wagers."

"Fell the champion? Can an ant fell a tree?" someone shouted, and the crowd shrieked with laughter.

"Pity the poor wee thing, Hercules, and throw him down now before he wearies," added another.

The two wrestlers edged around each other. The giant laughed as Fitz gamboled and jumped about. "Come here, you puny weakling, you grub. Hold still and let me fell you," the big man said.

"You wish to fell me? You must catch me first," Fitz growled.

"Nay, elven man, let us end this."

Fitz continued to caper and carry on. Finally the giant reached out one long arm, grabbed Fitz by his hair, and threw him down. Fitz landed on his knees but managed to keep his back and shoulders off the ground.

Will was torn. He relished the idea of the unpleasant little man thrown into the dirt, but Fitz was unfairly matched against the giant, and Will knew what it was to be small. "Take care, Fitz," he called finally and reluctantly. *"Cave et cura."*

The giant pushed Fitz with a great push that carried him into the watching crowd, and the crowd pushed him back. "Finish him, Long John," one man called, and another, "Finish him afore I am late for supper and you have to answer to my wife!"

Fitz would not be finished, but hopped and skipped about, taunting the big man. "I be lower to the ground than you and have not so far to fall, but you will topple like a tree," he roared.

The match went on and on, Fitz dancing around as the giant chased, wearying, moving ever slower. Finally the giant bent over to grab Fitz once again, but the little man scuttled away and ran between the giant's legs. He rammed his huge head into the back of the giant's right knee. When the leg bent, Fitz grabbed the enormous foot from behind and twisted it hard to the side. The giant toppled, and his shoulder hit the ground.

There was silence, and then the crowd erupted into whistles and shouts, hisses and jeers. Coins were collected from those who had placed their wagers on the wrong man, and half were poured into Fitz's hands.

Fitz limped away and Will ran after him. "Hoy, Fitz, hoy! What a spectacle!" Will twirled in glee. "You did teach the brute, Fitz, that you did!"

Wincing, Fitz wiped blood from the corner of his mouth. Will's forehead furrowed. "But you suffer such hurt and abuse. Is it as Master Tidball says, that you cannot help brawling? You have taken all my wages. Are you so greedy that you must wrestle for even more?"

Fitz stopped to replace his doublet and smooth his hair before he put his cap back on and limped forward. "Your wages? Tidball pays no wages, not to any, nary a penny. But someone must feed you and the girl and even me from time to time. She must have a new kirtle and cloak when she outgrows the old. Tidball does not see to that. Where do you think the coins come from?"

"Scurvy liar, I disbelieve you. Master Tidball gives you coins and you drink them away."

Fitz jingled his winnings. "Believe or disbelieve, we eat well tonight."

Will stopped still. "You mean 'tis true? Verily? You provide the sausages and ale and such for us? But Master Tidball—"

"The man is a nip-cheese. Also a scoundrel and a brute. Be watchful and wary and expect no good from him."

Master Tidball, Will realized, was indeed somewhat less kindhearted and friendly than he first seemed. He remembered the man's angry outbursts, his abuse of the girl, the cruel prank about the Black Dog. Could Fitz be telling the truth?

Fitz stretched, groaned, and sighed a mighty sigh for one so small.

"Have you pain?" Will asked him.

"Aye, but this pain will pass. Worse yet is that I miss my Cecily. She went a year ago to be with daughter Agnes when she had her child, and she has not come back. When she is not with me, I find myself ill-natured and spleeny." Fitz shook his great head.

That explained his disagreeableness, Will thought. Fitz had a family elsewhere and longed for them. "Did you not care to go also?" Will asked. "Master Tidball disfavors and derides you, and you owe him nothing."

"Indeed, but I could not leave the girl here with

him. She continues to defy him, and he will not stomach that for long. As yet he is bluster and threat, but I fear for her." Fitz wiped his face with his sleeve and spat. "She has no one but me to watch over her."

"Could you not go to your wife and take Grace with you? Or would your daughter be feared to look on her?"

"Nay, my tall, lovely daughter has looked on her mother and me all her life without fear or disgust," said Fitz. "She and her husband run an inn near King's Lynn, and certes they would welcome the girl. But she belongs to Tidball."

Fitz walked on, Will at his side. Will looked down at the little man. "Why, Fitz, I believe you have grown smaller."

"Nay, you ninny, you be taller than when first you came. Still a shrimp, but a somewhat taller shrimp."

Taller? He was taller? Will squared his shoulders. Mayhap he would not be a runt forever. He rubbed his chin hopefully, but it remained whiskerless.

They reached a small grove of trees and Fitz threw himself down. "Be off, Sparrow, and let me rest. I am too old to be earning money in this fashion. And watch out for Tidball," he added with a yawn. "He can be cruel."

"I have known worse," Will said. "My father were never a gentle man—he did like the sound of his fist thumping into something. But he was truly cruel only when cup-shot." Will paused, remembering. "At the end he were cup-shot all the time."

He stood a moment and studied Fitz's weary face. Ugly, yes, and disagreeable at times, frowning and scowling, but he was the one who cared for them all. And the girl trusted Fitz, turned to him for comfort. Certes he was not what he seemed. Was it ever so? Had Will never noticed?

The boy kicked a clod of dirt that proved to be a rock and shouted his pain to the world. Then he turned and left Fitz snoring beneath the tree.

EIGHTEEN

CONSIDERING WILL'S DECISION AND

ITS CONSEQUENCES

WILL WALKED aimlessly through the fair, for the first time heedless of the colors, the noise, the smells of baking pies and roasting meat. Head down, he was lost in thought. Fitz, the ugly little Fitz, had proved himself caring and brave. But what of Will himself? What was he? A liar and a thief, no good to anyone. He could do nothing for Samuel and the Duchess. Couldn't save Nell. When Grace was menaced by the young louts, he stood aside and apart. He wished to do so no longer and thought and thought about what he could do now.

Will returned at last to the wagon. "So, Sparrow, you have flown back to the nest. I should flog you away from here—it would be just as you deserve," said Master Tidball, watching the boy come, but he did not raise a hand. Will stood and scratched his nose and waited.

"I cannot rely on even one of you," Tidball went on. "Why, fairgoers have been in and out of the booth with no one watching. Any of them could have walked off with my treasures."

Aye, anyone who wanted a one-eyed pig or a pickled lizard, thought Will. *Not likely.* "I was distracted by the fair," he said, "and the hours passed. I pray your pardon."

Tidball grunted, which Will took to mean *Well, do not do so again.* "Lock the wild girl in the wagon," he said.

Grace wiped her hands on her skirt. "But I have had no supper."

"Nonetheless," said Tidball, "I have not forgotten your defiance." He nodded toward Will. "Sparrow, see to it."

Whistling, Will walked Grace to the wagon. As she climbed in, he whispered, "Be of good cheer, Grace Wyse. I have devised a plan that will please you and mightily displeasure Master Tidball. All will be well." He was rewarded with her smile, all the more lovely for being so rare.

Will heard someone call, "Ho, Baldhead! I know you be there!" and Master Tidball jumped to his feet. "I must be off," he said, and hobbled away.

Fitz appeared with cheese and bread and the leg of a roast goose. He unlocked the door to the wagon and handed Grace some supper. Will heard murmuring and even a bit of soft laughter before Fitz closed and barred the door again. He winked his bruised eye, and Will snickered. They sat to eat, leaning against the wagon. "How long have you been here with Tidball?" Will asked, his mouth full of goose.

"Cecily and I had been fair to fair many a year. She sang, I tumbled. When Tidball appeared some years ago with a wee mite of a kitten that proved to be a girl, we joined with him for her sake." Fitz frowned. "When Cecily left, I stayed, and you know the why of that."

"Tell me of your wife," Will said. "Is she . . . er, small, like you?"

"She be a mite smaller," said Fitz, and Will's eyes widened in wonderment. *A poppet, she must be, a fairy woman.* "Her voice be as sweet as an apple tart but she suffers no argument or disagreement. She makes the softest cakes, the sturdiest breads, and an eel stew that would charm the angels from the skies." He sighed.

"Now that your daughter has had her babe, Cecily can return here to be with you."

"Nay, she is now granny and will have no patience with oddities and prodigies. I pray I can go to her with time." Fitz crumpled his face in such a comic pantomime of woe that Will did not know whether to mourn with the little man or laugh. Fitz stood, yawned, and bade Will good night.

When Fitz was snoring loudly inside the oddities booth, Will crept to the wagon and unbarred the door. "Hist, Grace," he whispered. "'Tis time. We shall see the mermaid baby befittingly buried."

She emerged, rubbing her eyes, and said, "I knew you would help me . . . her . . . us. I knew it." And she rewarded Will with another smile.

They crept into the booth, careful not to alarm Fitz, who muttered and thrashed but did not wake. Moonlight streamed into the roofless booth and shimmered on the mermaid's bottle. Grace and Will each took a handle and lifted the flask. It was heavy and slippery and cumbersome but the two managed to carry it out of the booth and into the deserted fair.

"Have an eye to that stall, Grace!" Will muttered. "Look out!"

"I am being right careful but 'tis so heavy. Ow! Ow! You are leaving it all to me!"

"By my beard, you are—Why are you laughing?"

"You have no beard!"

"Well, did I have, I would swear by it that you are less help than a stewed prune. Now mark me, walk slowly and be still."

With grunts and groans, huffs and puffs, they carried the mermaid's flask through the fair to where the town turned to wildness. The flask glowed green in the leaf-filtered moonlight. Will shivered and his spine tingled. He looked about for fearsome things.

"Do you seek someone?" Grace asked him.

"'Tis just that I mislike the woods in darkness. Are you not afeared?"

"Nay."

"Not even a bit?"

"I like the darkness. I look like everyone else in the dark."

She was right, Will thought. She did look like everyone else, and he found he liked better her looking like Grace, odd though that might be. But he did not say so.

They put the flask down on the ground, and Will heaped mud and twigs over it.

"Nay," said Grace, "she must have a grave."

"A grave? She is in a bottle."

"She must be taken from the bottle and buried in a proper grave." Will was startled by the *whoop, whoop, whoo* of an owl, and his gut tilted and tumbled. "Grace, I am no gravedigger," he said, his voice but a squeak. "Let us go from this place. She is safe where she lies."

The girl stamped her foot, which made no sound there in the soft earth, but Will gave in. There would be a grave, a small grave but a proper one, for the mermaid baby. Grumbling, he found a likely digging stick and began. Grace could be tyrant indeed, Will said to himself, and he was happy he had not said the pleasant thing he had thought a moment before.

Grace squatted down beside him and dug with her hands. Finally they had a hole deep enough. Taking a stone, Will struck the bottle several times, and the glass shattered. The air grew rank with the smell of strong spirits and rot. Grace made a bed of moss in the hole, Will tipped the creature in, and they covered it with dirt and leaves, it being too late in the year for flowers.

"We should have a prayer," said Grace.

"Know you any?"

"Nay," she said.

So Will recited the Lord's Prayer, which he knew but did not know how he knew, for his father did not pray. They bowed their heads in silence for a moment. Then Grace said, "I have a prayer I just now made." She bowed her head again. "Sir God, I pray you accept the mermaid baby into Heaven. Never did she do a bad thing but made many people happy to look upon her for only one penny. Amen."

Grace and Will looked down at the mound under which the little mermaid lay, and Grace whispered, "Godspeed to you, baby."

Will gathered the shards of glass and dropped them into a hollow stump, lest some person or animal step on them unawares. Then they turned to go, picking their way slowly through the darkness, back toward the fair.

A sudden shaft of moonlight lit a lane where a deer stood, still as midnight. A young doe, by the look of her.

"Oh, Will," Grace whispered, "is she not beautiful?"

Will considered the deer. Soft reddish coat, large ears that twitched and twisted, eyes deep and dark in the moonlight. Aye, she was beautiful. Tasty, belike, and beautiful. She turned and bounded away.

"'Twould be wondrous, would it not, to live like a deer?" Grace said. "Eat berries and nuts, make a bed of soft grasses and moss, and sleep beneath the midnight sky."

"Nay, I be knowing something of that and 'tis not so wondrous. Moss makes you itchy, and the belly grows tired of berries."

Grace bent, picked up something from the path, and held it pinched between her fingers. A mushroom it was, pinkish, its cap spotted with white, tiny and perfect. "It looks like a wee fairy in a big hat." She smiled.

Will stared at Grace a moment. "You find such pleasure in small things. I am surprised, given your face and your fate and all."

Grace's lips closed in a pout, but then she said, "Pish, Sparrow, my face does not make deer less comely or my pleasures less sweet."

Grace knew how to juggle life, thought Will, near as well as Benjamin did. No matter her face, Grace would never be ordinary.

They crept back to the wagon. Will closed Grace inside and then crawled underneath to sleep. He thought of Grace, whose mother had sold her; of the mermaid baby, taken from its mother somewhere far away; of his own self, left by his mother. His mother . . . He felt the familiar grizzling in his liver.

The night was silent but for the wind in the trees and the distant hoot of an owl. He rolled out from under the wagon and paced about. He had so often pushed thoughts of his mother away that now he had trouble calling her to mind. It was so long ago. She wore blue, he remembered, and soft leather shoes with buckles, and she carried the scent of lavender. She smiled at him, cupped his chin and tousled his hair, sang to him at night.

A soft, moist breeze blew like a caress across his face. Will took a deep breath and let it out slowly. His mother—wherever she went, and why—must have loved him. He was not the reason she left, no matter what his father said. Will might be liar and thief, but he was not unlovable. And that was an entirely different pair of breeches, he thought. Entirely different. He crawled back under the wagon, clutched his few memories to him, and fell into a dreamless sleep.

"Awake, you sluggards, you knaves, you lazy curs!" Master Tidball shouted in the morning, long before the dew of dawn had dried on their backsides. "Tomorrow this fair will end. We will be on to Stourbridge!" Master Tidball clapped his hands. "Up now! Lure me some visitors! Astound the crowds! Earn pennies and more pennies!" He chirped and chuckled and twirled his walking stick.

"What and where might this Stourbridge be?" Will asked Fitz, who was standing before the booth.

Fitz yawned. "'Tis another fair, near to Cambridge."

"Phew, Fitz, turn your head aside lest your dragon breath burn my eyebrows off," Will said, just as Master Tidball proclaimed, "Not just another fair, Lancelot, you mindless minnow. The finest fair in England but for Bartlemas, and rich with fine goods—Italian silks and velvets, wine from Spain, furs and amber from the Baltic, precious books and painted dishes, silver spoons and rings of gold."

"What matters that to us?" Will asked. "Since my promised wages have failed to appear, I cannot buy even last week's cabbage."

"Such a fine fair will countenance no ordinary oddities," said Master Tidball, ignoring Will's grumble. "We must be peerless, incomparable, a truly transcendent troupe of prodigies and marvels. I have at last persuaded Benjamin to join us. A blind juggler. Imagine." He did a careful little dance step. "Now if the creature would but pace and roar, if you, Lancelot, you gargoyle, you eyesore, would wear a hat with bells, tumble, and walk on your hands like a proper dwarf, we would be a true company of wonders. Our fortunes would be made, and then next, London and Bartlemas Fair—the most splendid fair of all!" He spun his walking stick once more and lifted it like a sword before him. "Aye, London, you oddities and prodigies! London!"

The man removed his cap and scratched his bald head. "Perhaps you, Sparrow," he said finally, "when we reach Stourbridge, could do something clever. Mayhap you can tumble? Twist your body into unnatural shapes? Walk on your hands? Eat fire or swallow swords? Make eggs disappear or coins appear?"

Will shook his head no and no and no.

"Bah," said Tidball. He narrowed his eyes and examined the boy as if by close scrutiny he might yet determine some talent or deformity hitherto unknown even to Will himself.

Master Tidball unlocked the wagon and let Grace

out. "Before we go to Stourbridge, we must add to our little band of oddities. You, wild girl, take these eggs and shake them, hard, like this."

Grace took the basket he handed her. She looked at him and furrowed her brow. "Their insides become confused," Master Tidball explained, "and with luck the chickens that emerge will be odd-looking indeed. Fine additions to my collection." He shook one of the eggs violently. Grace took one and softly turned it over and back.

"Nay, stupid girl, shake it hard, like this." Master Tidball took the egg from her and gave it a ferocious shake. He grinned at Grace's look of disgust and dismay.

As Tidball turned away, Grace winked at Will. She cradled two of the eggs and murmured, "Grow, little chicks, into fine fat fowl with sensible insides."

"Sparrow, give extra food to the chicken," Tidball went on, "to plump her up. Then join Fitzgeoffrey, who will be seeing to the oddities inside. Some are looking a bit tattered and untidy. We cannot allow that at Stourbridge fair. They must be extraordinary, worth a penny to see."

After the chicken was fed, Will joined Fitz in the booth. "How," Will asked him, "did Master Tidball come by these treasures?"

Fitz snorted. "Treasures? What treasures?"

Will gestured toward the unicorn skull. "Such as this."

Fitz snorted again. "The knave fastened a horn onto a goat skull. And look closely at the bits and pieces of fish and bird bones that he calls a sea monster. Treasures, indeed. The man is a rogue and a craven counterfeit."

Will looked closer at the unicorn skull. Was it in truth a goat and no unicorn at all? His mind reeled. Master Tidball passing off a goat as a unicorn and Grace Wyse as both wild girl and wild cat? Even Will had never thought to tell lies as big as that.

"I cannot find the mermaid," Fitz called to Tidball, and suddenly Will remembered the deeds of last night. His face grew clammy and his hands trembled.

"Fitzgeoffrey, you beef-witted toad," Tidball roared as he came into the booth, "you are useless as a hat full of holes. I would send you away this minute if it did not amuse me to abuse you."

Fitz glowered and his ears glowed red, but he looked again through the booth. Will felt a fluttering in his belly. He feared what was coming and, to forestall it, joined the fruitless search.

"Why are you not helping, wild cat?" Tidball asked Grace, who had come in and was standing silently to the side. "Know you something?"

She looked down at her feet.

"Tell me!"

She said nothing.

"Since you will not speak, I shall lay a punishment upon this wretch—the worthless Lancelot Fitzgeoffrey— for I put him in charge of my marvels. 'Tis his fault she is missing, and he shall be thrashed for it." He grasped Fitz's arm and pulled him close.

"Nay," Grace whispered. "You cannot punish Fitz for this."

"Say not *cannot* to me! I can do whatever I like, thrash whomever I choose!" Tidball twisted Fitz's arm, and the little man yelped.

"But 'twas my doing. My idea and my plan," Grace said.

Tidball loosed Fitz and swung to face Grace. "What have you done? Where is she?"

"She is gone. I knew she did not like being in a bottle. She was in part a person, after all. So I dug a hole and buried her, as was right and—"

"You simpleton!" Tidball swung his stick against a turtle shell, and the sound reverberated in the booth. "She was no part person, but made of cat skull and fish tail, sea grass and pretense. I can easily construct another." He peered at her. Will could see him thinking. "How, pray, did you take her? Are you sure 'twas you?

You were locked in the wagon. And the flask was too heavy for one to carry."

Master Tidball turned and loomed over Will. "You, Sparrow, was it you?" he growled. "Did you steal my mermaid? I shall have the watch on you, and you shall rot in prison until your nose falls off your face."

Will opened his mouth—to say what, he did not know—but Grace shook her head. "No," she whispered to him. "No." So he said nothing.

Master Tidball grabbed Grace by the arm. "You, then," he said to her as he pulled her from the booth and pushed her into the wagon. "Ungrateful brat." Will heard a thud and a cry, and then another. "I will think of a suitable punishment for you, you ugly, unnatural creature, and you shall stay locked in here until I do!" Tidball burst from the wagon, slipped the bar across the door, and stormed off, brandishing his walking stick like a cudgel.

Fitz moved to stop him. "Stay back, Fitzgeoffrey," Tidball shouted as he stalked away, "lest I grind you into the mud."

Will pounded the wagon until his fist throbbed with pain. What an addlehead he was! All these weeks he had chosen to believe that the ugly, misshapen Fitz was a villain and that Tidball's guileless blue eyes and easy laugh betokened a good and generous nature. He pounded the wagon again. But that was not the way of it. Fitz had told the truth. Tidball was the villain, the greedy one, the thief, the liar, the brute. As Fitz climbed into the wagon to see to Grace, Will shook his head.

Certes, things are not what they seem.

NINETEEN

HOW WILL HATCHES AN ENTERTAINMENT,

DELIVERANCE, AND TROUBLE

I T WAS the last day of the fair. Grace stayed locked in the wagon. While Fitz collected pennies at the booth, Will called people to come to the wonder room one last time. Still furious—at Tidball and at himself—he spent his anger in mocking Tidball, mimicking his limp and his clumsy dancing, swinging a make-believe cudgel, and shouting, "Lancelot, you gargoyle, you insect, you beef-witted toad!" He found that fairgoers appreciated the foolishness and followed him, laughing, to the oddities booth.

When evening came, Fitz was not to be found. Master Tidball told Will, "We leave for Stourbridge at dawn tomorrow. I have important business in town and will not return until morning. You and that trustless troll have us packed and ready to go." Master Tidball looked at the wagon. "And do not free the wild girl, nor feed her, for she continues to defy me. Let her feel the pangs of hunger, the ugly, ungrateful wretch." He left, twirling his walking stick and humming.

Now that he knew what he knew of the odious Tidball, should Will quit him? he wondered. Go from here, even without his wages? But to leave Grace and Fitz behind . . . What could be done? What would deliver all three of them?

Despite, or mayhap because of, Tidball's harsh commands, Will let Grace out of the wagon. "You must ne'er tell Master Tidball about your part in burying the mermaid baby," she told Will. "Aye, he will punish me, but if he learns of your part in the burial, he will beat you most severely and turn you out. Promise me you will not tell him. Promise."

Will nodded.

Grace helped Will pack up the oddities, ready for stowing in the wagon at first light. He built a fire, and they drew near it for warmth. Lights from the fires of other fair workers twinkled, and there was music and the smell of food cooking.

Fitz returned anon, one eye blackened, but he must have gotten the best of his opponent, for he dropped an armload of onions, bread, and wedges of crumbly yellow cheese into Grace's lap. "Eat, my children," he said, and he fell to the ground with an *ooof.*

"*Salvete,*" said a voice. "Greetings, my friends."

"Benjamin! At last! Sit, sit!" said Fitz.

Benjamin sat. "I have decided to travel with you as far as Stourbridge. And then? *Ignoro,* I do not know, but I will juggle what comes."

"Have you yet been to Stourbridge fair, Master Juggler?" asked Grace, her mouth full of bread.

"Aye, 'tis most glorious—a feast of revelry and merriment, music and laughter, sumptuous smells and tastes, and crowds not miserly with their coins. I am certain you will find it colorful and altogether splendid to see."

"I fear all I shall see is the inside of the wagon," Grace said. "Master Tidball is becoming ever more insistent that I play the wild girl, and I cannot. I will not." She shuddered.

Benjamin gestured helplessly. "My lovely Grace, I wish we could rescue you from your captor as Saint George rescued the princess from the dragon."

"My dragon walks on two feet and swings a mighty cudgel."

"Indeed," said Benjamin.

Will leaned forward. "Imagine this: if we were to depart from here while Tidball is in town? Hitch Solomon to the wagon and go—to Stourbridge or elsewhere—and Tidball would come back to find no one and nothing." Will snickered at the thought.

"Aye," said Fitz, his chuckles growing to gusts of laughter. "He would strut about, swinging his stick, shouting 'Paltry moldwarp' and 'Puny minnow' and 'Ugly creature' all he wished, and we would not be here to hear him. 'Twould be most satisfactory, would it not?"

"Aye," they all agreed. "Most satisfactory."

Grace passed a wedge of cheese to Benjamin, who cut a slice for himself and passed his knife to Will.

"Cut some of that onion for me, stripling," said Fitz.

Will stabbed the blade into the onion and held it up before him. "Nay, nay, eat me not," he said, bobbing it around, "for I am Master Tidball!"

"Aye!" said Fitz. "'Tis Baldhead to the life!"

Will grinned. He held the knife and the onion aloft. "Yea, in sooth I am the evil-hearted Thomas Tidball, bald of head and bitter of heart, sly-minded knave and insolent villain, teller of lies, torturer of innocent maidens, and creator of false oddities."

Will nodded to the puppet. "Master Tidball, I did it, I, Will Sparrow. I helped Grace bury your false baby mermaid, and I wished 'twere you beneath the ground." He lowered his voice and spoke as Tidball: "Oh crows and daws! Plagues and madness! A burning Devil take you, you puny, peevish schoolboy! Begone from me! Avaunt! Aroint! Before I flame in rage, set you afire, and sup on your roasted ribs!"

Laughter overtook them.

Said Benjamin, "This paltry juggler cannot observe the Tidball poppet but can recognize him by his unpleasant nature, which even a blind man can see." He threw a crumb of cheese toward the puppet.

"Had we a pea or a walnut," said Fitz, "we could make a Fitz puppet to battle the evil Tidball."

Waggling the onion-headed puppet toward Fitz, Will shouted, "Lancelot Fitzgeoffrey, you drunken brawler! Weak and writhled shrimp! Lord of the minnows! I will crush you and use your bones to powder my bottom!"

Fitz added in a Tidball voice, "Now, come and do all the work, buy all the food, and take no wages."

"And stop being kind to the wild girl," Grace put in.

"You must do as I say, lest I grind you into the dirt," said Will, brandishing make-believe Tidball. "And I say polish my boots with your tongue, fetch me a barrel of ale, and sing for me, you tiny, tuneless drone. Lancelot Fitzgeoffrey, give us a song!"

Fitz began a popular tune that Will knew well:

> We be soldiers three—
> *Pardona moy je vous en pree—*

Lately come forth of the low country
With never a penny of money.

Benjamin pulled his flute from his bag and tootled along as Grace and Will joined Fitz to sing the verse again. At the rare sounds of music and laughter from the oddities, a few folks from neighboring fires began to gather.

"Now," cried Will, "Tidball must sing." The onion puppet bowed to left and right, cleared its throat, and sang:

Thomas Tidball is who I be—
Pardona moy je vous en pree—
Master of these persons three
With never a penny of money.

"Aye," shouted the gorbellied purveyor of pies, puddings, and pancakes, standing near the fire, "'tis him indeed, the varlet. He borrowed three shillings from me and now pretends not to know me."

"He owes me a shilling still from a bout of knucklebones at the inn," said the metalsmith.

"And me, who bested him at primero!" called another voice.

So that was where their wages went, Will thought. Tidball had gambled them away. And much more, it seemed.

The Tidball puppet grumbled, "Hush, knaves. There is more to my song:

> Tidball is who I be.
> Come work for me or play with me.
> But you'll get more coins from yonder tree,
> For I've never a penny of money.

His listeners laughed and cheered. Some of them, brimming with ale and celebrating the end of the fair, threw pennies. Pennies! Will scooped them up and said to Fitz, "Know you what these are? Deliverance."

"You be taking those pennies and leaving us?" said Fitz.

"Nay," said Will. "Not my deliverance. Grace's. And yours."

Fitz clapped Will's shoulder but said, "Even if Tidball wished to sell her, those pennies are not enough."

"Added to what you win by wrestling?"

"We need to eat."

"Fitz, listen well to me. We will eat less. We will make a puppet play to share with visitors to the Stourbridge fair and keep the pennies we collect. Tidball need not know."

Will dribbled the coins into Fitz's hands, but Fitz shook his head uncertainly.

Someone pulled on Will's sleeve. "I have a puppet, too," said Grace. She held aloft an apple impaled on a stick. "'Tis me," she said. "An apple-cheeked maiden at last. Make Tidball talk to me."

And the Tidball puppet growled, "You, wild girl, you ungrateful wench, do something fierce!"

Sheltered by her cloak, Grace held the apple puppet up. "Fierce, aye. Fiercely will I punish you for your evil ways, you terrible Tidball." Her thumb and first finger held a twig, with which she began to beat the Tidball puppet. "A whack for your greed!" she cried. "A whack for your selfishness! A whack for your cruelty!" The Tidball puppet whimpered and fled, and the Grace puppet bowed in triumph.

The audience cheered again and threw more pennies. Fitz put them into his pouch.

Will brought the onion Tidball back and sang again, and the onlookers joined in:

> Thomas Tidball is who I be—
> *Pardona moy je vous en pree—*
> Master of these persons three
> With never a penny of money.

"Thus we repay the terrible Tidball!" someone shouted, and there was more laughter.

At the edge of the audience, Will's eye fell on a face that was not laughing.

Tidball!

Will's heart thumped in his chest. What did the man here? Had he heard everything? As Will struggled to contain his panic, he saw Tidball turn and disappear.

Grace clutched Will's jerkin. "Did he hear us?" she whispered.

Will shrugged. "Belike." He exchanged glances with Fitz, and the three stood together in silence. Benjamin tootled on as if all were well. Presently the audience, with the sudden halt to the merriment, drifted away, and the only sound left was the soft melody of Benjamin's flute.

"What?" he finally asked. "Why the quiet? Has something happened?"

"Tidball was here," Will said.

"Here?" Benjamin shook his head. "Woe and lacka-day, that bodes not well."

Will agreed. He thought of Samuel's riddle—if you bite an onion, it will bite you back. Will pulled the onion off the knife and threw it into the fire. They could but wait for Tidball's bite. Will feared it would be terrible.

TWENTY

OF MASTER TIDBALL'S HEAD AND

WILL SPARROW'S FEET

A SOFT BUT steady dawn rain washed clean the stalls and wagons of the fair, turned dusty paths into slippery sewers, and dripped maddeningly onto the fair folk as they readied their departure.

Will, Fitz, and Benjamin stood in soggy silence. The fair was over, first light had come and gone, and still Tidball was not to be seen. "What shall we do now?" Will asked.

"We can only do what we know to do," said Fitz with a shrug. So Benjamin went to an open space behind the ale stall to practice, and Fitz and Will packed the oddities and prodigies into the wagon, dismantled the booth, and fastened it to the top. Lest Tidball return and find her free, Grace squeezed herself into the wagon between a giant turtle shell and the head of the one-eyed pig.

"You fetch us something to break our fast," Fitz told Will when all was in readiness, "and I will fetch Benjamin."

Most of the food vendors had packed up and left, but finally, at the far end of the market square, Will found a baker's stall. The oven had cooled, so there was no fresh bread, and Will had to be satisfied with a loaf left from yestermorn with but a few mouse nibbles. He then stopped at the ale stall for a small pail of watery beer and turned for the wagon.

The wagon? The wagon! He looked around in shock. Where was the wagon? Will's head swiveled furiously, but he saw no wagon. It was like his jest of the night before except that he, not Tidball, was the one returning to find the wagon gone. And Grace! Was Grace in the wagon and gone too?

"Master Brewer," Will called to the man tending the ale stall, "did you see Tidball's wagon depart? Or hear it? Did the girl perchance climb out before it left?"

The man shook his head and shrugged.

Will visited the few booths and stalls left near the oddities booth, but it was fruitless. No one had seen Tidball or the girl in the blue cloak, nor could they tell the sound of one wagon from another.

An archer with his quiver on his back was striding past, and Will asked him as well. "Aye," the man said. "I walked with Thomas from the inn but moments ago. He said he was come to fetch the wild girl and take her back to the inn. Said he had sold her."

"Sold her! Nay, he would not," Will said, but his heart began to thump. Doubtless he would, the scurvy knave!

Will ran behind the ale stall. "Fitz!" he cried. "To me! To me!" He grabbed the little man by the shoulder. "Tidball has sold Grace! Sold her! They have gone to the inn."

Fitz's cheeks paled, his eyes bulged, and without a word he raced past Will.

Benjamin took Will's arm, and they followed the little man, tripping and slipping in the mud. "I fear he is punishing her for our mockery," Will said. "'Tis my fault! Mine!"

The three skidded to a stop in the inn yard: the wagon was not there. Had the bargain been completed and everyone scattered? Will's heart thumped even louder.

From the stables behind the inn rang frantic cries, and they hurried in that direction. There was Tidball, pulling Grace by the arm into the stables, though she kicked and fought.

"Stop, Tidball, you villain!" Fitz roared.

Holding Grace fast, Tidball looked them over, his face twisted in scorn. "You three ungrateful louts," he said, "get you gone. I want nothing more to do with you." He held tightly to his walking stick with one hand and Grace's arm with the other. Pull and tug as she might, Grace could not escape. "The wild girl's new owner will be here in a moment. He will not be as gentle and generous with her as I have been."

"Nay, you venomous toad!" shouted Fitz. "You shall not use her thus, scurvy, barbarous brute!" He lunged at Tidball and grabbed him around the waist. Letting Grace loose, Master Tidball lifted his walking stick and struck Fitz again and again. The girl cowered against the wall as the air rang with the sound of whacks and wallops.

"Nay, Thomas, nay!" Benjamin called out. "Whatever violence you be doing, cease!"

The little man fell to the ground, and Master Tidball kept striking him. Will watched in horror. Fitz was a skilled fair wrestler, but he was no match for an enraged man with a stout stick.

"Stop!" Grace cried, lunging at Tidball. "Stop! No more! I will go wherever you wish and do whatever you command. I will go willingly to a new owner. I will hiss like a cat or bay like a hound. Just do not hurt Fitz anymore!" She pulled on Master Tidball's arm. Whirling, he backhanded her across the face. She flew and crashed into the stable door.

Angry blood pounded in Will's ears. In a fury he charged Tidball and caught hold of his arm. The man lifted the stick to swing at Will, but Will grabbed it and held on. Tidball twisted the stick violently, and Will fell. Then, remembering Fitz and the giant, Will scrambled to his feet, ran behind Tidball, pulled up his unhurt foot, and twisted. Tidball tottered unsteadily on his injured leg for a moment and then toppled to the ground, where he lay still, a jagged rock beneath his head, blood oozing.

Fitz struggled to his feet, helped Grace rise, and took her by the hand. All three stood and looked down while Benjamin repeated, "What? What? Is it over? How fare you all?"

"Is he dead?" Grace asked.

"Oh, fire and brimstone!" said Fitz in a hoarse whisper. "Dead."

"Dead? Who is dead?" asked Benjamin. "Quickly, tell me!"

"'Tis Master Tidball," said Grace in a small, tight voice.

"And he is dead? *Ei, ei, ei,*" Benjamin said, shaking

his head in dismay. "We must have the sheriff. Belike someone will hang for this."

Dead? The sheriff? Hang? *He* would hang! Will's heart gave one huge thump and then started beating wildly. And he ran as if the Devil were on his tail, through the town, back toward the fair.

Dead. The man was dead. The bailiff would be called, and the sheriff, and Will would be blamed. Ah, woe! His neck would be stretched, and his body left hanging on the gibbet for crows to pick at. He dashed tears of fear and guilt and self-pity from his eyes as he ran past the ale stall and the pastry shop.

Or . . . would the others be blamed? Would the law take Fitz and Grace and punish them? There would be no one to speak up for them, tell the sheriff the wicked thing Tidball had done, selling Grace like a wheel of cheese, and how they were just trying to protect her. He slowed as he ran behind the toy seller and the pewter-smith, through the archery range.

Fitz and Grace were oddities, easy to accuse. Will's face flushed with shame. He had left them to take the blame. But he cared for no one but himself, did he not?

When he reached the road from Ely, he stopped to catch his breath. The fens lay ahead, he thought, and then . . . and then . . . Where would he go? He was, as

Grace had called him, a pitiful stray. He had joined them because he needed them, and he knew it. And they knew it and allowed him to stay.

He turned and began the trek back to town to face whatever would come. He left the road to cross the bit of woodland where he and Grace had taken the Duchess. What would Samuel think of him now—a murderer? And he passed through the clearing where Fitz had wrestled for their suppers.

More than once Will stopped to turn and run again, but he did not, though his steps grew leaden and slow. His shoulders were heavy with fear, dread, and shame, although he felt, too, a small measure of pride.

The rain had stopped before he reached the market square. Wagons moved to and fro, pack horses whinnied, merchants shouted and argued and called farewell. All was hurly-burly.

Where were Fitz and Benjamin and Grace? Had the sheriff come and taken them? If so, how could Will discover where they had gone? His mouth was dry with fear.

"Will Sparrow, open your eyes," he heard someone call. He whirled around. There at the side of the road sat an odd-looking trio: a very small man with yellow hair and great bushy eyebrows, a threadbare fellow tossing a ball from hand to hand, and a creature with a friendly cat face wrapped in a blue cloak. Rips and muddy smears marred their clothing, but their faces were bright.

"We knew you would come back," said Grace, and she smiled a smile that lit the gray day and put Will in mind of silver bells and honey cake.

"Why? How?" he asked. "I left you to take the blame."

"You would ne'er abandon us," said Grace.

"But I did."

Grace stood up, brushed mud and leaves from her cloak, and put her hand into Will's. "Nay, you came back, just as we knew you would. You have had enough of running."

Will stood still for a moment, experiencing the unfamiliar warmth of another's hand in his. He left it there and turned to Fitz. The little man's face was bruised and his lip bloodied.

"How do you, Fitz?" Will asked.

Fitz smiled. He was missing another tooth. "My pains are but trifling things compared to my joy."

"Joy? How so joy?" Will asked him. "Where have they taken Tidball? And what is to happen to us?"

"He were not dead, young Sparrow," Fitz said. Will huffed in astonishment. "He slept as if dead for a wee time and then awoke with an aching head and a raging temper. I told him you had run and taken the girl with you."

"But I did not."

"No, you did not. I had her hidden behind the stables. And his walking stick also, lest he thought to cudgel me again. He raged about duty and debt and ingratitude and then washed his hands of the lot of us. Said he was finished with odd folk and henceforth would traffic only in bird bones and turtle shells. And he raced away as fast as Solomon could go." Fitz stuck his legs out in front of him and smiled a smile full of pride and relief. "Did you not see him on the road?"

"Nay," said Will. "I came another way."

Grace was laughing. "The last time Master Tidball himself drove the wagon, he raged so at sheep blocking the road that he fell from the seat, injured his arm, and twisted his ankle."

"In good sooth? That was the accident that led him to hire me?"

"Aye, and a happy accident indeed, for it brought you to us." Grace squeezed his hand.

Benjamin and Fitz stood. "We are free now," said Fitz, "to live upon our own."

"I am for Stourbridge, Fitz," Benjamin said. "Belike you and the girl could go along. Be who you are and profit by it. Share your takings with no one."

Fitz raised his eyebrows and looked at Grace. She shook her head. "Nay, I think we are finished with fairs," he said. "We are people, not exhibitions. We will make an ordinary life in King's Lynn with my wife and daughter."

Benjamin nodded and said, "Doubtless 'tis best. But I will venture on. *Carpe diem,* seize the day; fortune favors the brave. I am off for new places and adventures."

Will looked at the chill gray sky and then down at his ill-gotten jerkin. He pulled the jerkin off and slipped it into Benjamin's sack. It was not an action he was accustomed to, putting something *into* a sack.

Fitz added a handful of coins. "Stay on this main road," he said to the juggler, "and likely you will find a fair-bound company to travel with."

"*Valete, valete,* farewell," Benjamin said, with a salute to his cap, "*ab imo pectore,* from my heart. God keep you, Fitz."

Grace took Tidball's walking stick from behind her and handed it to Benjamin. "I shall miss you, Sir Juggler."

"And I you, Grace. Be of good cheer, my lovely. Remember, as the ancients said, *suum cuique pulchritudine,* to each his own beauty. And you, Will Sparrow, fare you well. *Ne obliviscaris,* do not forget all we spoke of. Learn how to juggle life." He began his trek down the path away from the fair, so surefooted and certain that for a moment Will wondered if his sight had been miraculously restored.

"Best we start also," said Fitz as he looked at the sky.

Grace stepped forward. She had the three-legged chicken on a leash of red ribbon. As she pulled the hood of her blue cloak over her head, Fitz turned and looked at Will. "And you, boy?"

And Will walked right up to them as if he belonged there. Which, he supposed, he did. Oddities, all of them—a liar and thief, a disagreeable little man, and a girl with the face of a cat—belonging nowhere but with each other.

"I still have the coins thrown at the Tidball puppet last night," Fitz said to Will. "Before we leave, I think Master Tidball ought to buy you boots. King's Lynn is some days' walk from here."

A spark of hope, a small thing but true, crept into Will's chest. A home and safety. Might he stay there long enough to grow tall? And chin whiskers? And Fitz's sweet-voiced Cecily—might she be kind and soft and, well, motherly? And boots. Boots! Will wiggled his toes in glee and looked down the road that lay ahead.

AUTHOR'S NOTE

When I decided to write a book about a child in Elizabethan England who runs away and joins a troupe of "oddities and prodigies" traveling from fair to fair, I knew the child had to be a boy. In the often brutal sixteenth century, a girl on the road would not have long survived. And I did not believe a girl could successfully disguise herself as a boy in a world with so little privacy. So the child had to be a boy—my first major boy character. That took a lot of thinking, research into young male behavior, and input from my editor, but I finally developed a character who seemed to fit. And I set him on the road to the fair.

Many of us have enjoyed recreations of medieval or Renaissance fairs with their costumes, flowery "Milady"-laden language, quaffing mugs, and roasted turkey legs. These fairs, alive with music and dance, archers and knights on horseback, are based on the traditional fairs of medieval and Renaissance England, equally colorful, raucous, and outrageous.

Fairs have a long history in England. There is conjecture that Neolithic sites of 4000–3000 B.C.E. were in fact a sort of fairgrounds for the trading of pelts and primitive tools. Many fairs developed as temporary markets where goods, livestock, and produce were sold or traded, and people traveled, sometimes for many days, to meet those they needed to buy from or sell to.

The number of fairs increased dramatically after the Norman Conquest in 1066. Between 1199 and 1350, more than 1,500 charters or royal decrees were given to lords of the manor or dignitaries of the church, permitting them to stage fairs and markets for the trading of goods and the celebration of feast days.

A fair was usually tied to a specific Christian religious occasion, particularly the anniversary of the dedication of a church. Such fairs might then continue annually, usually on the feast day of the patron saint to whom the church was dedicated, and last from one day to many weeks. This custom was kept up until the reign of Henry VI (1422–1461), by which time a great many fairs were kept on these festivals—for example, at Smithfield in London on St. Bartholomew's day (the famous Bartholomew, or Bartlemas, Fair attended by the diarist Samuel Pepys and dreamed of by Master Tidball). Over the centuries, when the rivers in England froze hard enough to support traffic, frost fairs were celebrated on the ice. During the winter of 1564–65, the Thames River froze, and Londoners could enjoy archery and football and dancing on the ice, vendors' booths, and performances. Even Queen Elizabeth I visited that fair.

Exhibitions at fairs sometimes included what were called oddities or prodigies, displayed in a sort of sideshow. People are often fascinated by anything different or unexpected, and fairs provided plenty of examples: two-headed cows, conjoined pig fetuses, dwarfs and giants and albinos, and creatures such as sea monsters and beasts from foreign lands, many of them as false as Tidball's mermaid.

The seventeenth century was the heyday of prodigies and oddities. James Paris du Plessis produced an early chronicle of these exhibits, an unpublished three-hundred-page book entitled *A Short History of Human Prodigies and Monstrous Births, of Dwarfs, Sleepers, Giants, Strongmen, Hermaphrodites, Numberous Births, and Extreme Old Age, Etc.*

The diaries of Samuel Pepys (1633–1703) describe yearly visits to St. Bartholomew's Fair, where he saw monkeys dancing on the rope, a goose with four feet and a cock with three, a legless man who danced on his hands, and other oddities.

The oddity Grace Wyse was inspired by the portrait of Antonietta Gonzales (1552–1614) on the cover of *The Marvelous Hairy Girls* by Merry Wiesner-Hanks. Antonietta, her father, and most of her brothers and sisters suffered from hypertrichosis, an extremely rare genetic condition that made them unusually hairy. There have been fifty documented cases worldwide since the sixteenth century. The Gonzales family is probably the most famous because of the number of paintings, books, and medical case histories that feature them. Unlike most people marked with such irregularities, the family was not shunned or mocked; they dressed in ruffs and elaborate jewel-trimmed gowns and were welcome visitors in the courts of Europe, though sometimes treated more like pets than people.

Duchess, the learned pig, is also based on a real individual. In the sixteenth century, Londoners flocked to see "Marocco, the thinking horse," who, among his other talents, could total figures on dice, count coins, and identify playing cards. If a horse could, could a pig? I wondered. Indeed. A learned pig, taught to respond to commands in such a way that it seemed able to answer questions by picking up cards in its mouth, caused a sensation in London during the 1780s. The pig even had its own song—"The Wonderful Pig." Sheet music could be bought for only sixpence. In New England in 1798, William Frederick Pinchbeck displayed a "Pig of Knowledge" who could read, spell, tell time, and distinguish ladies from gentlemen. The original learned pigs were followed by other trained pigs, which subsequently became a feature of fairs and other public attractions in Europe and America into the nineteenth century. Shamu the whale and his relatives are modern examples of amazing trained animals.

Today attitudes toward people who are different in any way are more humane and more respectful. So-called freak shows fortunately are things of the past. And modern medicine can solve many of the problems and cure many of the disorders that led to people being classed as oddities.

In a world with no radios, CD players, or iPods, music was mostly something people made themselves for themselves. The songs in *Will Sparrow's Road,* whether just titles or full lyrics, are all traditional ballads or drinking songs from the sixteenth century, although at times Will makes up his own words. The songs sung in the book are "Barbra Allen," "The Wee Wee Man," "Greensleeves," "Tomorrow the Fox Will Come to Town," and "We Be Soldiers Three." Most people were familiar with them, and illustrated broadsides with the words and/or music could be had for a penny. Many of these songs are still sung today, although there is much variation in words and melodies.

Benjamin's Latin is as correct as I, nearly fifty years after my last Latin class, could make it. Tobias's incantation, however—*Hey fortuna, numquam credo, passe, passe, et flotatus, fugit, fugit, levitatus!*—is a mix of ungrammatical Latin words commanding the egg to rise and fly.

Tobacco was new to England in the sixteenth century, although it had long been used in the Americas. English and European explorers introduced the practice of smoking, or "drinking smoke," to their homelands when they returned. In England most men used simple white clay pipes, and pipe parts are still sometimes found in the mud along the Thames River in London.

The "wicked Irish" that Will imagines himself riding against were those fighting for Irish independence in what was called the Nine Years' War (1594–1603) against English rule. The struggle did not end with the end of the war.

If you want to read more novels set in this time period, try these books:

Blackwood, Gary. *The Shakespeare Stealer; Shakespeare's Scribe; Shakespeare's Spy*

Cheaney, J. B. *The Playmaker; The True Prince*

Crowley, Suzanne. *The Stolen One*

Hassinger, Peter. *Shakespeare's Daughter*

Hooper, Mary. *At the House of the Magician; The Betrayal; By Royal Command*

Horowitz, Anthony. *The Devil and his Boy*

Kolosov, Jacqueline. *The Red Queen's Daughter; A Sweet Disorder*

Meyer, Carolyn. *Loving Will Shakespeare*

Rinaldi, Ann. *The Redheaded Princess*

Sutcliff, Rosemary. *Brother Dusty-Feet*

Thomas, Jane Resh. *The Counterfeit Princess*

Wrede, Patricia. *Snow White and Rose Red*

Selected Resources:

Addison, William Wilkinson. *English Fairs and Markets.* London: B. T. Batsford,1953.

Bates, A. W. "Birth Defects Described in Elizabethan Ballads." *Journal of the Royal Society of Medicine* 93 (2000):202–7.

Bondeson, Jan. *The Feejee Mermaid and Other Essays in Natural and Unnatural History.* Ithaca, N.Y.: Cornell University Press, 1999.

Cameron, David Kerr. *The English Fair.* Thrupp, U.K.: Sutton, 1998.

Crystal, David, and Ben Crystal. *Shakespeare's Words: A Glossary and Language Companion.* London: Penguin, 2002.

Gazetteer of Markets and Fairs in England and Wales to 1516. www.history.ac.uk/cmh/gaz/gazweb1.html.

Jay, Ricky. *Learned Pigs & Fireproof Women.* New York: Villard, 1986.

Malcolmson, Robert, and Stephanos Mastoris. *The English Pig: A History.* London: Hambledon, 1998.

Pepys, Samuel. *Diary.* www.pepysdiary.com.

Singman, Jeffrey L. *Daily Life in Elizabethan England.* Westport, Conn.: Greenwood, 1995.

Strutt, Joseph. *Sports and Pastimes of the People of England from the Earliest Period.* On www.sacred-texts.com/neu/eng/index.htm.

Thomson, Rosemarie Garland, ed. *Freakery: Cultural Spectacles of the Extraordinary Body.* New York: New York University Press, 1996.

Wiesner-Hanks, Merry. *The Marvelous Hairy Girls: The Gonzales Sisters and Their Worlds.* New Haven: Yale University Press, 2009.